FRIENDED

A NOSTALGIA SONGFIC

KILBY BLADES

For permission requests and other inquiries, the publisher, Luxe Publishing, the independent publishing label of independent author, Kilby Blades, can be reached at: info@luxepress.net.

ISBN: 978-0-9991532-5-3

For all of those who came before me.

PART ONE
LITTLE EARTHQUAKES

ONE

LITTLE EARTHQUAKES

Oh, these little earthquakes.
Here we go again.
Oh, these little earthquakes.
Doesn't take much to rip us into pieces.
-Tori Amos, *Little Earthquakes*

ROXY

I picked up my phone to read the tweet that had announced itself with a melodic chime.

@OfficialStarVega: Just put some video of Adam's party online.

Thanks, Mom, I thought, rolling my eyes as I threw my phone back onto the table. Since my mom had become quasi-famous, she was abusing the hell out of social media: posting stuff on YouTube, going overboard with Instagram selfies, and insisting I follow her on Twitter. Unable to be bothered, I turned my attention back to my Hulu show and bowl of Cap'n Crunch. It was the first Saturday in weeks that my dad had gone fishing, the first Saturday I wouldn't have to endure hours of *Love it or List It* reruns on HGTV, the first Saturday I didn't have to work on some lame school project. Fuck if I wasn't going to watch as much *Project Runway* as I wanted.

Since leaving my mother to life on the road and moving back to Rye, I'd found relish in things other teenagers took for granted. All my life I'd been the parent—running the household and cobbling together a decent education while she gigged and auditioned her way toward rock star dreams. She'd been tearful in that typical way of hers, and "so heartbroken" that she had to go on tour—that her big break as a backup singer for Selfish Bliss meant leaving me in the care of my father. Never mind its dubious coincidence with her engagement to Adam Jinn, Selfish Bliss's lead singer.

The rambling speech that followed had been utterly unnecessary. Her engagement was a bigger break for me than it was for her. I still hadn't forgiven the stunt she'd pulled a year earlier: moving us into Adam's beach bungalow two months after she met him; forcing me to leave my friends and change schools. Since then, I'd pretty much been counting the days until I'd be on my own. The proposal had been a stroke of luck for both of us. I loved my mother, but I was grateful to live with my dad.

There had been arrangements to make, of course. Summer visitation with my father had been changed to sole custody. Years of legal separation culminated, finally, in divorce. I didn't know the full story behind my parents' custody battles over the years— only that my dad had tried to see me more, that they'd fought about it, and that he'd always failed. Tucked under his arm, shared relief had been palpable as we'd watched my mother's limo disappear.

Six months later, my dad was still overcompensating—giving me all the breaks that came with normal teenage life. He barely let me lift a finger, except to cook a few times a week. He'd helped me design a new bedroom set that he'd had custom-built at his shop, and let me pick out accent pieces for the rest of the house that made it feel like my own. He maintained his truck, paid the bills, and kept the house in good repair. Nothing said "normal teenage life" like days like today: five consecutive hours watching TV in my pajamas and pocket money on the kitchen table.

Two root beers, a pack of Skittles, and half a bag of Funyuns into the afternoon, I headed for the shower so as not to be late for Zoë. Her favorite boutique was getting new arrivals, and she'd recruited me for the pilgrimage to Littleton. I preferred a good vintage store or thrift shop to any boutique—somewhere I could find something original. Plus, having money for new clothes was, well...new.

From that first day at Trinity High when she'd plopped down next to me in Spanish, Zoë had informed me that we'd be friends. Judging from her blue lipstick and unicorn hair, I'd believed her. It had been a bold move—just because we were the two people at Trinity who looked least like we belonged there didn't mean we were the same flavor of misfit—but freakishly confident was just how Zoë was.

Zoë was also freakishly rich, and it still surprised me a little that we got along so well. Rich kids had never been my crowd. Half of what I'd hated about living with Adam had been the kids in Orange County. I'd have taken bonfires on the beach with my crew from Long Beach any day over getting drunk at house parties with top-shelf liquor from someone's parents' stash.

After pulling on a pair of skinny jeans, a snug white long-sleeved tee, and a cropped black leather jacket I loved, I brushed out my shower-damp hair and inspected my function-over-fashion array of beanies. The indoctrinated knew that there were two Californias: Northern and Southern were different in every way. And this L.A. girl still hadn't gotten used to the Northern California cold.

I headed downstairs to look for my fashion-over-function

sunglasses. I didn't care that it got so overcast here in the winter that my dark glasses practically rendered me blind. A glance at the microwave clock told me I had five minutes to kill. I cracked my laptop open at the same time I cracked open another can of root beer, and hit all of my usual sites. Some time between watching my mom's video and snickering at the stupid-ass "single and ready to mingle" meme the class clown, Dutton, posted on Instagram, I noticed that I had a new friend request.

Huh.

It wasn't that I didn't have friends, mind you. Just that everyone I knew—my loose clique in Rye, my old crew from Long Beach, my mom, my dad, and my cousins—was already connected to me. I was still wracking my brain to figure out who would have asked for access to my private account when a tap of my finger showed me the last profile pic I expected to see. I choked on the soda I was attempting to swallow, sputtering root beer ungracefully through my nostrils.

Jagger fucking Monroe?

Still coughing a little, I closed my eyes and tried to even my breathing. When I reopened them, the friend request was still there. His too-perfect face, and his hipster name and even his handle mocked me: @moves_like_jagga. I looked between the "Confirm" and "Ignore" buttons once. Twice. Three times. The sexy but standoffish Jag Monroe was friending *me* on Instagram? The same Jag Monroe whose cold shoulder froze me out of my seat every day in Civics class?

"Roxy?" Zoë's quasi-frantic voice called from the hallway.

I hadn't even heard her open the door. Shaking my head to snap myself out of my trance, I looked up from my computer. She strode in noisily, the teal swatch in her hair slightly greener than the blue of her suede tassel boots.

"What's going on?" she demanded. "I was knocking for, like, five minutes."

A guilty glance at the top right screen of my Mac Book confirmed that I'd been staring at the friend request for at least ten.

"Sorry..." I mumbled, still dazed.

I pushed the laptop towards her, not yet trusting myself to comment. She slid into the kitchen chair next to mine, and when her eyes fell upon the screen, they widened considerably. I braced myself for an ear-splitting, high-pitched trill.

"Since when are you friends with Jag Monroe?"

I felt more like myself when my eyes rolled of their own volition and a snarky retort rolled off my tongue.

"Yeah, we Netflix and chilled last night..."

Zoë didn't flinch.

"Well, don't you want to be?" she demanded.

The question was purely rhetorical. Anyone who said they didn't want a piece of Jagger Monroe was surely lying. His sage-colored eyes, that silken voice, and the sumptuous aroma that wafted around him drew man, woman and child into his orbit. Yet, the only thing as certain as his magnetic pull was the finality of your position around him. And me? I wasn't even in the Jagger solar system.

I must've spaced again because, suddenly, Zoë was reaching for the laptop. I surprised myself by the speed with which I swatted her hand away.

"I can't confirm his friend request!"

"And, just what is stopping you? He is a total fox."

I stifled a groan. Zoë was so used to getting what she wanted that limits were an abstract concept to her. She didn't understand how different life was for people like me. I was cautious...circumspect...skeptical of innocent explanations. I knew that sometimes the light at the end of a tunnel was a train.

"Zoë..." I said in the voice I reserved for small children, "... people like me are not friends with people like Jagger. And, even if we were, we wouldn't have gotten that way by confirming a friend request on Instagram."

"But—"

"It's a joke."

Speaking the words stung me, even though they were true.

"Roxx—"

"Forget about it, Zoë. I have."

And I hit the 'Ignore' button. And that was that.

———

JAGGER (THE PREVIOUS NIGHT)

Declan's obnoxious cackle overtook my room, earning a distracted wince from noise-sensitive Gunther and a sideways glare from me.

"Goddamn, bro. These girls are finger-lickin' hot for you!"

Ever since Declan got with Annika Smith, he'd been living the single life vicariously through us, his two best friends, and since Gunther was not-so-clandestinely in love with Zoë DuBois, that pretty much left me.

"Which one?" I asked absently, too comfortable in my zero gravity chair to muster any real interest.

Declan sat across the room at my enormous computer desk, the pièce de résistance that started us calling my room the bat cave. Whereas most kids had modest rooms with a respectable bed, some shelves for books, and maybe a TV, my room was tricked out with a California King, a full living area with sofa and chairs, and professional-grade computer equipment that I used for music editing. I did alright at downplaying how rich my parents were most of the time, but my room totally incriminated me.

Our Friday night ritual of video games and bong hits had been bastardized by Declan's new hobby—trolling my Instagram account. It didn't help that it was Gunther's turn to pick the game this month. "Civil War: A Nation Divided" was no "Guitar Hero", and stopping to strategize every five minutes was killing my buzz.

"Lauren Calloway, dude. She just PM'ed you a picture of her in a thong. And that Victoria chick sent you a link. She wants you to take the 'What is Your Sex Color?' quiz. Hers is vermillion," Declan murmured, waggling his eyebrows.

Ugh, gross.

"Jag—what is your favorite command?" Declan asked in a teacher-like voice, ""Obey", "please", "now", or "follow"?'"

"It's "shut up", you dickwad," I said, throwing a lighter at his head. He'd better not be filling out that fucking quiz.

Even after we resumed the game, I was still a little disturbed. I only got on Instagram in the first place because my cousins from Oregon kept bugging me about it. At the beginning, accepting follow requests from people at school had seemed benign enough. By the time I figured out that half the school was treating it like some sleazy internet pick-up site, it was already too late. I wondered whether you could un-friend people...

"So, Deck...what's Annika up to, tonight?"

I swear, 'obvious' is Gunther's middle name.

"Roller derby, same as always..." Declan said, too innocently.

Yeah—practice with the same team that Zoë DuBois just *happened* to be on.

"Huh," Gunther uttered, pretending he was just making conversation.

He was too easy a target for Declan not to throw a curveball. I waited for it.

"Yeah, she said tonight was a special practice—bikini pudding-wrestling, or some shit."

Gunther blanched. I bit the inside of my cheek to keep from laughing. It didn't make any sense to begin with, and if it were true, Declan sure as shit wouldn't be here with us.

"We should go to her next bout," I suggested helpfully, throwing Gunther a wink. "I dig girls in booty shorts."

Gunther looked relieved.

"They're up against Littleton three weeks from Saturday," Declan offered knowingly. "We should definitely go."

Yeah—we so had our boy's back.

"Roxy'll probably be there, too," Declan continued, clearly for my benefit.

Meddlesome prick.

"Jesus Christ, Deck," I mutter with as much annoyance as I can muster, "...I help her clumsy ass off the cafeteria floor one goddamned time, and you think I'm in love with the girl."

Declan could give lessons in the righteously indignant eyebrow arch.

"It's more than you've ever done for any other girl at Trinity High."

Benedict Gunther shrugged affirmatively.

"Come on, man..." I muttered in my get serious voice, "If I went spreading that Prince Valiant shit around, they wouldn't stop with e-mailing me pictures of their tits. They'd be coming to my fucking house!"

I only needed to see the look on Declan's face to know the "t-word" worked.

"Dude, who sent you pictures of their tits?"

"No one you need to be thinkin' about, son," Gunther piped up. "Annika'd kick you from here to Sunday."

Declan dropped it because Gunther was right. Annika scared the hell out of everyone. Problem solved and bacon saved. For now.

TWO
FRIDAY I'M IN LOVE

I don't care if Monday's blue,
Tuesday's gray, and Wednesday too.
Thursday I don't care about you,
but Friday I'm in love.
-The Cure, *Friday I'm in Love*

ROXY

"Forget about it, Zoë. I have."

My own lie played on a loop in my head. But days went by and I didn't forget about it, not that Zoë would let me.

She spent part of Sunday doing recon on who else at Trinity High was Instagram friends with Jagger. By Monday morning, she was in full spy mode, with feathered hair like one of Charlie's Angels as she surreptitiously studied him in the parking lot, cafeteria and quad from behind dark sunglasses. She spent until Friday trying to convince me that Jagger was checking me out just as stealthily as she was him. But, the fact that he had been as standoffish as ever in Civics reinforced what I already knew: none of it was for real.

Friday night I went to roller derby practice with Zoë—and when I say "went to practice" I mean "stood on the side of the rink eating Skittles and trying to avoid injury". With the bowling alley and the diner as the only other hangouts in Rye, I didn't have anything better to do. It wasn't the first time I'd tagged along, nor was it the first time I'd observed their game with feigned disinterest. Privately, I was fascinated by the girls on her team. They were like Amazon women: tall, coordinated, and muscular, whereas I was short, clumsy and trim in a decidedly non-athletic way.

But my ulterior motive—watching Zoë like a hawk—had to do with her teammate and secret acquaintance, Annika Smith. The same Annika Smith who was dating Declan McCabe, one-third of the Bod Squad and close associate of Jagger Monroe. Annika was tough as nails and solitary somehow, even though she captained the derby team and was joined at the hip with Declan at school. She'd been cool with Zoë for all two years they'd been on the team, though they never spoke at school and never hung out. She was into cars and had even restored the black 1973 Camaro she was famous for driving herself and helped fixed cars at her older brothers' body shop.

Zoë meant well, but was prone to interloping. Asking about Jagger would spark curiosity as to why Zoë was asking. The last thing I needed was for Zoë to mine information from a comrade who would figure it out.

"So, Jag's not seeing anyone...", Zoë mentioned casually on the ride back to her place after roller derby was done.

I grimaced. Some job I'd done on Zoë control.

"No wonder," I turned the heat as high as it would go and raised my palms to let them hover over the vents. "He spends all his time stalking strangers on Instagram."

"He likes you..." Zoë was indignant.

"Based on what? Things you won't shut up about now but never mentioned before?"

I had her there. All week, Zoë had been making mountains out of molehills, insisting that he looked at me, reading significance into the one time he'd helped me off of the floor. The cafeteria thing was ancient history, and even if it wasn't, the lack of acknowledgment since that day rendered any earlier acknowledgment null and void. And so what if he looked? He didn't, by the way, but a lot of people had at some point. That was what happened when you were a new girl in a small town that had its teeth in the juicier morsels of your family's business. I was Luke Vega's daughter and Adam Jinn's soon-to-be stepdaughter. Of course people were going to look.

"He likes you, Roxx..." Zoë practically whined. And since I'd run out of responses for her provocations...

"Kind of like Gunther likes you?"

Zoë swallowed whatever she'd been ready to say.

It was after ten-thirty when we got back to her place; Zoë lived on the edge of town in one of the post-modern beauties near the top of River Road. Rye had become an enclave for a certain class of Californian. A flattering photo spread published in a travel magazine years before had showcased our pristine redwood forests and clear lakes, putting my parents' little hometown on the map. The accompanying article had lauded its lack of through traffic, several celebrated artists in residence, and its quaint downtown. It had been bait to the city-dwelling ultra-rich who were ready for an alternative or who simply wanted an idyllic place to build a second home.

Zoë's parents definitely fell into this category. Her dad had been employee number ten with one of the big Silicon Valley tech giants. Other transplants had similar stories—of cashing out and getting out of the rat race farther south. Zoë hadn't moved to Rye until she was eleven. Like Zoë, the cohort of kids at Trinity who hadn't been born here all had bigger houses and drove nicer cars. Not everyone who'd lived here since forever liked the way the town was changing, but the influx was good for business for people like my dad.

Zoë jumped in the shower while I got into my pajamas. I wandered down to the kitchen to grab us some drinks, stopping to admire my father's custom craftsmanship. My dad had hand-made the cabinets in this and half of the high-end kitchens for miles around. When I was little, he'd been known only locally, but commissions throughout Trinity County had led to commissions in Humboldt and Sonoma. Getting noticed in Marin had naturally led to clients in San Francisco and Silicon Valley. His work had gone into homes featured in Architectural Digest and on TV.

Heading back upstairs, I unlocked my screen to thumb through my phone. I'd checked it in the car, but who knew what I'd missed? When Zoë found me ten minutes later, I was exactly as I had been the previous week. This time, my hand trembled as I handed her my phone. Her eyes widened as they fell upon Jagger's image on the screen. That enigmatic fuck had friended me *again*.

"Why is he doing this?" My voice was a whisper. My gaze switched between the two buttons that had haunted my thoughts.

Confirm or deny?

Confirm or deny?

"There's only one way you'll know for sure."

Zoë looked up from the screen with a question in her eyes. This time, I had to know the answer. This time, I didn't stop her from hitting "Confirm".

———

JAGGER

I grabbed a bowl, some milk, and a half-empty box of Golden Grahams, and toted them up to my room. Gunther and Deck had just gone home, and, at 12:30AM, I had the munchies. I settled at my desk to surf my regular sites—I hadn't gotten a turn with my own computer in hours, what with Declan's greedy consumption of what Annika forbade him. The few glances I stole throughout the night found him viewing my Instagram feed, what looked like pole dancing on YouTube, and some pretty freaky porn.

Going straight to Instagram, I figured I'd better assess the damage right away. It had taken me a few days this week to figure out that Deck hadn't been a passive observer during last week's spree. Not only had he viewed some of the crazy ass messages I got from girls—he'd responded to a few of them.

I looked in my sent messages and was relieved to find nothing I hadn't written myself. A few people had hearted snarky responses to posts he'd written on my behalf. I didn't like him posing as me, but at least nothing too out of character had emerged. After reading a few status updates, I was about to move off of Instagram completely when my eye caught something under Recent Activity:

Roxy Vega started following you.

Wait...what? When had Roxy friended me, and when had I accepted? My account was private and so was hers. So what if I knew that because I'd had the impulse to check it out a time or two? It took me a second to figure it out, and when I did, I was livid.

"Son of a bitch..." I growled.

Declan and his theories about my alleged crush on Roxy Vega. This time he took things too fucking far.

THREE
IT'S A FIRE

'Cause this life is a farce.
I can't breathe through
this mask, like a fool.
So breathe on, sister breathe on.
-Portishead, *It's a Fire*

JAGGER

After I called Declan and tore him a new one, sleep was no longer an option. The only shows on at two-in-the-morning were infomercials, I was maxed out on video games, and my piano would wake up my parents. Not that I really wanted to do any of those things, anyway. In the solitude of my room there was no point in denying that I was desperate to know everything there was to know about Roxy Vega.

Sure, Declan had it coming for pimping me out on Instagram. But some secret part of me cheered his interference, despite the resulting mess. His overture had stayed true to the Jagger Monroe persona—abrupt, impersonal, maybe a little cocky. Only he and Gunther knew how greatly my assholery had been exaggerated.

I had a bit of a reputation—one I came by honestly—one that had never died. It didn't matter how far in the past it was. Being caught in flagrante delicto with anyone would've been a notch in any Freshman's belt: I was caught at the biggest party of the year losing my virginity to the Homecoming Queen. Not only did that little stunt secure my status as a sex god, it sent the stock of everyone I was friends with soaring. By sophomore year, Gunther, Declan and I were among the most popular kids in school.

Even the teachers treated us differently. We could get away with anything, and for awhile we did. Then Michelle Peters happened. Turns out that being a guy and a manwhore is a respectable profession according to the rules of high school. It also turns out that if you're a girl, and you *date* a manwhore, everyone calls you a slut. The bitterness that came from that realization only dug me deeper. I seemed more the part now that I was a misanthropic prick.

So, yeah. My plan was to hang with my bros and ride out high school, get good grades, and re-invent myself at the college of my choice. People still thought whatever they wanted to about me, and I still stood by and let them. But I'd never planned on liking a girl. I'd never planned on Roxy Vega.

I barely knew anything about her—only that she was different. She'd been born here, but not being raised here...well, it showed. Most kids in Rye dressed like they spent entire weekends at the mall begging the people at Forever 21 to shut up and take their money. Most girls wore too much make up—eye shadow and blush and some sort of fairy dust that made their faces shiny. Apart from her hallmark—a single, bold stroke of color on her lips—Roxy was fresh-faced and wore clothes that hadn't come from any mall. Between the leather jackets and dark, metallic nail polish, her look was kind of edgy, but it never seemed like she was trying too hard. It was a good sign that she was friends with Zoë DuBois—one of the only other originals at Trinity High.

I clicked on Roxy's name and it took me to her page. Did I mention she was kind of beautiful? In her profile picture, her bone-straight, strawberry-blonde hair was down, thick and shiny over one shoulder. Her cheeks flushed pink on her heart-shaped face, their apples the same dusty rose as her cupid's bow lips. She wore a Van Halen t-shirt—one that looked like it had actually been purchased in 1980, its neckline cut out to reveal a smooth, slender shoulder. And, her eyes—those deep brown pools of mystery—pinned me with an emotion I could not identify.

Goddamn.

Scrolling through her feed, it made my heart skip a little to find so many posts about music—*real* music. Nothing about that band her mother was supposedly on tour with, thank God—Selfish Bliss sucked. No, her feed was chock-full of references to original music—not the over-produced, derivative shit that tried to pass. As the son of a retired music producer, I'd heard a lecture or fifty about the evils of the pop music industrial complex. The indignity of engineering hits with mediocre artists rather than making magic with real talent was exactly why my mom had gotten out.

Scrolling lower, I scanned for selfies. I both loved and hated that I found none. It was a bit stalker-ish, but I took to looking for photos she was tagged in. At school, I could barely steal tiny glances, but the novelty of staring as long as I wanted found me feasting on what I saw: Roxy in cutoffs and Chuck Taylors, laughing with friends; Roxy on the beach at a bonfire, her tiny frame tucked under the arm of a big, older-looking boy; Roxy posing with a woman whose likeness was so strong, she had to be her mother; Roxy holding a guitar in the desert.

Every photo revealed something new and fascinating about this girl—something that deepened my ache to know more. But getting closer than this would be a bad idea. She was already on the fringes, already too different from everyone else, already too uncomfortable from their stares and whispers about her sudden reappearance and her L.A. style.

No, I resolved. My reasons for avoiding the Trinity High social scene were good ones, and my reasons for avoiding Roxy were better. I drew attention to everyone around me, and not the good kind. It would be reckless for me to do that to someone so private—someone so new she couldn't fathom the consequences. As far as she knew, I'd friended her, which meant she might have ideas. I had to stop them now, no matter how intriguing she was.

————

ROXY

I felt pathetic as I turned my attention away from my history essay yet again, palmed my phone and pushed my Instagram feed. I'd turned into one of *those teenagers* who could barely function without knowing every piece of news the second that it happened. Except nothing ever happened in Rye, and I was barely friends with enough people at Trinity to be involved in any sort of drama.

You're totally stalking him.

I totally wasn't—at least that was what I kept telling the voice in my head. I'd bet money that twenty or more girls at Trinity High—and probably a few boys—had taken their time admiring pictures of him. And the more I looked, the more I fixated on all there was to admire: it was hard to argue with tall stature, muscular forearms, and always-shiny-perfectly-tousled hair.

I don't know what I'd expected from accepting his friend request, though any attention seemed unlikely at this point. He hadn't commented on any of my posts and he still ignored me so hard in civics, I'd started to think he was getting extra credit from

Mr. McAbee for not speaking a word to me. How likely was it that he would even say hello before the end of the quarter?

Not any less likely than the friend request, Roxy...

Awesome—I was talking to myself again. And I was beginning to sound like Zoë.

Speculation would get me nowhere. And it could be that me thinking of him differently was exactly what he wanted. But I had to rely on what I definitively knew: Jag Monroe may be wickedly smart and undeniably pretty, but there was nothing cute about being rich and aloof. Sure, he tried to seem deep in that brooding kind of way that made lesser girls swoon—and swoon they did. But I had his number. Jag Monroe was shallower than a kiddie pool.

I'd seen enough movies to know what happened when the most popular boy in school turned his attention on the new girl, especially when rumor had it that said new girl was a prude. The fact that I hadn't hooked up with anyone at Trinity in the six months I'd been there had earned me that reputation. The male chauvinist rules of high school dictated a repulsive reward: elevated status for anyone who could break that trend.

No doubt, Jagger would expect me to be flattered that someone so inherently divine would give a second glance to someone so far on the fringes of the Trinity social elite. He'd only need to string me along briefly—to make me believe we were friends—would only need to take me on one sorry excuse for a date before he'd flash me a panty-dropping smile and achieve just that: a quickie in the backseat of the car his daddy bought him and the silent treatment from there to eternity.

But what if he really isn't that guy? screamed the wicked voice in my head—the one that wanted to believe that beneath his bad boy ways, there lived something good. He listened to music obsessively—in his car, in the library, and even tucked away in random nooks and crannies around school. And it was more than just having his headphones on. I'd caught him hanging outside of classroom doors as the bell rang, staying with his music until his song ended, looking raw as he got lost in something real. It was the one vice I held in common with my mother—one that would surely get me into trouble, as it had her—I was drawn to dark, tortured men.

Just as I went to put my phone down, the app reloaded and pushed new photos onto my feed. I recognized the posting style of an account I followed religiously. It ripped lines from old songs and arranged them to look like a guitar. People guessed the song and the artist in the comments. Eager to see whether I could guess, I took a closer look at the quoted lyrics:

> *Oh, and twisted thoughts that spin 'round*
> *my head*
> *I'm spinning, oh, I'm spinning*
> *How quick the sun can drop away*
> *And now my bitter hands cradle broken glass of*
> *what was everything.*

I read it twice. Three times. It sounded familiar but I couldn't place it. It wasn't until I tried to click into the comments to see what other people had guessed that I realized that the post was not the original. This post had no comments, only the repost symbol that showed that it had been taken from the original feed I also followed. The re-poster was none other than Jagger Monroe.

Holy shit.

It was nothing like any of the last dozen status updates he'd written. His older ones were all stupid captions and pictures he took at his house, things like "*Jagger Monroe is kicking shit-talkers' asses at Guitar Hero*" and "*Jagger Monroe is studiously ignoring his homework.*" I wanted to dismiss this strange message as random. So why couldn't some part of me shake the idea that it wasn't?

For minutes I sat, trying not to overanalyze the fact that the only things that had changed on his profile in the past few days were the cryptic nature of his updates and becoming friends with me. Half an hour passed. An hour. And I still couldn't stop myself from wondering. I was always wearing band t-shirts. Of all the things Jagger Monroe could know about me without actually knowing me, my love for music would be at the top of the list. Suddenly, he was posting song lyrics. The question now was, why? Was he speaking to me? Could he possibly be speaking to me?

FOUR

DRIFT AWAY

Give me the beat, boys and free my soul.
I want to get lost in your rock 'n roll
and drift away.
-Dobie Gray, *Drift Away*

JAGGER

Declan had the good sense to look sheepish as he stepped into my car on Monday. Between giving him the silent treatment for the entire weekend and our stilted conversation on the way to Gunther's, he'd gotten the message loud and clear. I felt slightly guilty for letting him suffer, but he had to know I was serious about him backing off. His intentions were good, but there were things even he didn't know.

We took our places in the parking lot, our cars near the main doors of the school. Gunther and I leaned against the back of my Tiguan and Declan bent over Annika's Camaro. Ostensibly, we were just enjoying our freedom until the five-minute bell rang. The truth was, Gunther never went inside 'till he'd laid eyes on Zoë, and we still had a few minutes to wait.

Being with Gunther was always easy—the guy only had three quiet moods. Intense Gunther was reserved for war games and Zoë. Calm Gunther was the norm, a perfect counter balance to Declan's and my extremes. And droll Gunther—who didn't come around nearly enough—was my favorite.

"Looks like you got Deck more nervous than a long-tailed cat in a room full of rocking chairs..."

I had to crack a smile at that. The accent he put on when he spoke his southernisms was so good you'd think he grew up in Alabama rather than just spending summers there with his grandma.

"What the hell happened with you two anyway?"

By then, my annoyance over Declan's prank was fading and the reality of my new circumstances was closing in. The truth was, I was dying to talk to someone. And, his own situation notwithstanding, Gunther tended to be wise about such things.

"Roxy Vega and I are friends on Instagram."

Gunther's voice returned to its natural accent, though surprise made it register a bit high.

"Since when?"

He ripped his eyes from the driveway long enough to shoot me a curious glance.

"Since Declan friended her from my account."

His eyes widened momentarily before returning to the road to scan for Zoë's orange Cayenne.

"What are you gonna—"

He stopped short the moment he saw Zoë, the surprise in his eyes replaced by the predicted stare of longing and sharp intake of breath. I was also preoccupied, because barely a school day had passed since Roxy's arrival to Trinity that Zoë hadn't been her ride.

Instead of chancing a glance in their direction, I changed the subject and dropped a question about Redbone, the newest addition to the Emory household. Gunther kind of had a thing for dogs. I figured the lazy smile that came over his face any time he talked about his puppy would ingratiate him to Zoë more than the half-scared, half-constipated look he usually got when she was around. I listened with one ear as the five-minute bell sounded and students walked past us, up the steps, and into the main door.

Judging by the pounding of my heart as I realized my new "friend" would be passing soon, some part of me realized I was at least half as screwed as Gunther. He was busy waxing poetic about how protective his older dog, Beaufort, was of Red when a shy, melodic voice lifted over his.

"Morning, Gunther."

I looked up in shock at Zoë's unprecedented greeting, inadvertently catching the last glimmer of her Gunther-focused smile as she turned to walk inside and leave my slack-jawed friend in her wake. Roxy, for her part, was looking at me from behind her sunglasses, her cheeks beautifully flushed and her smile warm as she shifted her gaze to Zoë, then to Gunther, before continuing toward the steps. Gunther's hand and half of his body weight fell against my arm for support.

"She spoke to me..." he said with wonder, his eyes suddenly bright with hope as he watched her disappear through the doors. He blinked at least twice before turning his gaze back to mine. "Dude, did you see that? She spoke to me!"

Declan and Annika were suddenly next to us, supplying enough congratulatory snark to relieve me of the pressure to answer. But my pleasure at being smiled upon by Roxy was short-lived as I mentally replayed her expression. Hers had been a cryptic smile, maybe a calculating one. Coming up blank on what she could be scheming, a sickening possibility hit: what if Roxy accepting my friend request had nothing to do with me?

No.

My dawning theory shouldn't have bothered me. My dawning theory was kind of sweet. Because what if she thought I'd friended her in anticipation of the uniting of our cliques? It would have been as obvious to her as it was to me that Gunther and Zoë would end up together. What if her mysterious smile had just been a wink and a nudge—from wingwoman to wingman—in solidarity to unite our clueless friends?

———

ROXY

Thank God Zoë suggested cutting for lunch. She claimed that after the "good morning" victory with Gunther, she didn't want to run into him at school for fear of being overexposed. I listened good-naturedly over a personal pan pizza as she dreamily relived the look in his eyes—his answering smile to her call.

Zoë had spent half the weekend thinking she was pep-talking me into figuring out what was really going on with Jagger. If you ask me, she'd been building her own confidence to finally make a move. I was happy for her. That weird, pained look Gunther got around her-and-only-her was a dead giveaway. Any idiot could see how much he liked her. Any idiot but Zoë, that was.

Zoë prattled on about Gunther on our way back to school. I thought ahead to what might happen in Civics—to all the promises I'd made myself over the weekend about what would definitely *not* happen there. I would neither seem too interested, nor too eager, nor too impressed by anything about him because no, I didn't have a thing for Jagger.

So why were my hands fiddling with the zipper of my hoodie as I walked, too-slowly, to class? And what had I been thinking as I'd gotten dressed that morning? It had taken me 'till last night to figure out the cryptic post that had gone up on his feed some time on Saturday: the lyrics from an old Pearl Jam song. I mean, how many high school kids were into Pearl Jam? Sure, *I* loved them. Growing up with a musician mom who sang cover songs in nostalgia bands pretty much guaranteed the musical diet I'd been raised on was different from that of my peers. But what was Jagger doing reposting emo lyrics to a song written before he was born?

I'd pulled up the song: *Black*. I'd put it on repeat. I'd tried to piece together what he'd been thinking with that post. He might have strutted around like he was too good for everyone else—like he was God's gift to the world, and the school—but he was different when he listened to his music. These lyrics spoke of longing, of restless nostalgia for something or someone. Fuck if I hadn't wanted to know what music he listened to, in quiet places, in the shadows. And fuck if the lyrics didn't corroborate it. If I was honest with myself, it had been this hidden side of him that intrigued me. There had always been something sad about Jag Monroe.

"Hey..." he mumbled, barely looking at me as I slid into my chair.

"Hey," I offered.

It was two words more than we usually shared.

Mr. McAbee launched into his lecture. I was too preoccupied to hear. All of this was warping my perspective. They had only been hellos: Zoë's to Gunther and now, his to me. Why did some part of me want to re-cast him in this play? It all came back to the lyrics. Replaying them in my mind with him sitting right next to me worried at my stomach like my fingers worried at the zipper of my hoodie. Beneath said hoodie was the best I'd been able to come up with after overthinking things for a solid thirty-six hours. If his posting had been a call for attention, my vintage Pearl Jam Vitalogy tour t-shirt would be my reply.

"Miss Vega?"

Shit.

If Mr. McAbee was using that tone, he'd already asked twice. A not-so-subtle gape at the whiteboard offered me no clues. In a divine act of grace, the period bell rang. Kids sprung from their chairs, as if they'd been coiled and waiting to bound forth at the slightest signal. Mr. McAbee's "Pay attention next time, Roxanne" was issued sternly enough, but barely audible above the scraping of stools. The motion of Jagger rising to his feet and sweeping his books in to his backpack proved that he smelled as good as he always did.

A beat too late, I, too, sprang from my chair, still a little off-guard and momentarily forgetful of my hoodie. That is, until Jagger's eyes were suddenly glued to my chest. He recovered quickly, mumbling a goodbye before hastening out the door.

He saw it, I realized, with sickening doubt about my plan, *He saw my Pearl Jam shirt.*

It wasn't supposed to happen like that. I'd thought he'd drop a compliment, or at least that we would share a knowing glance, like in the movies. He wasn't supposed to be spooked by it, but I was pretty sure I'd scared him away.

Oh, God.

I zombied through the rest of the day—through class, then homework, then dinner with my dad. I took a long, hot bath, and distracted myself with some Ray Bradbury (no love stories tonight). The effort it took to not look at my phone during all that time was herculean. By ten-thirty, I was ready to rip it—the Band Aid had to come off.

Pushing my Instagram feed, I braced myself for his update, certain I would find something like *Anyone looking for a new Civics partner?* or *Just put out a restraining order on Roxy Vega.* Or, maybe the ultimate slap in the face: an un-friend. I clicked on his profile to see his recent activity. In place of a creepy stalker meme, I saw an album cover I easily recognized in a photo Jagger must have taken himself. It was an impressive shot: an angled sample of his face appeared in the bottom left corner. Huge headphones covered his ears. The half of his lips that you could see were upturned in a subtle smile. He was lying down and next to him on the floor was a vinyl record: *Binaural*. His post was hash tagged only twice.

#AmListening #pearljam

Fuck. Me.

FIVE

CALL ME MAYBE

Hey, I just met you and this is crazy.
But here's my number, so call me maybe.
It's hard to look right at you, baby.
But here's my number, so call me maybe.
-Carly Rae Jepsen, *Call Me Maybe*

JAGGER

She fucking got it. Roxy got the Pearl Jam reference. I'd spent half the weekend figuring out how to ward her off, but she'd treated my danger warning like a beacon. The pained song lyrics were intended to be both obscure and slightly frightening, to make her forget whatever compelled her to accept the friend request and to show her a side of me that would send her running. But she hadn't run-she'd come closer. The recognition in her eyes and the gorgeous blush on her cheeks when she saw me notice her shirt proved at least that.

I knew it had been extreme—and presumptuous—to think she would read into what I wrote at all. That I'd gotten so unhinged from thinking about her had only strengthened my resolve to keep my distance. By Sunday morning I'd formulated the plan; by midday I'd picked out the song and posted the update; judging by the silence of my usual stalkers on Sunday afternoon and evening I was pleased to believe it was scaring off more than just Roxy. And when she hadn't un-friended me by 7AM on Monday, I figured I might get away with admiring her from afar.

But, now everything was different. Now, she'd seen right through me and held out her hand. Now, Zoë and Gunther were that much closer to starting something that would make it hard for me to avoid Roxy. Now, I had a decision to make: step back or step forward? And it took me all night to decide. If anyone asked, I'd deny that I'd used a selfie stick and spent thirty minutes getting the right shot.

Of course, Declan was the first one to comment on the photo of me with my headphones on and the LP jacket sitting next to me.

Really, dude...Pearl Jam?

I rolled my eyes as I clicked reply.

You left your Spice Girls CD in my car. Again. #TrinHighRye

That's right—I hash-tagged that shit. Since obsessing over Roxy's possible reaction was the fastest way to insanity, I logged off for awhile. A hot shower, a fruitless tinker on my piano, and a lengthy session with my trusty companion, Spotify, were fitting distractions. By eleven-thirty, I had crafted a new playlist called "Beautiful", and couldn't resist hitting Instagram one last time. If she'd hearted my post, it would be a win.

I didn't even make it to checking my updates. A second before tapping the alert, a new posting from Roxy loaded at the top of my feed. The image had a simple black background, a thin, all-caps font, and a pair of silver and white earbuds dangling off to the side, framing the centered question: *What song are you listening to?*

The fingers of the hand that wasn't holding my phone carded through my hair. I blew out a long breath as I stared at the image on the screen. Not in any of the 217 posts that Roxy had made over the past two years had she once posed a question. A few people had already commented.

@DerbyGirlZoe– Rihanna: "Love on the Brain"

@OfficialStarVega – Does Adam's snoring count as a song?

@OliviaB$ – Adele: "Rolling in the Deep"

@CivilWarBuff$ – Waylon Jennings: "Mommas, Don't Let Your Babies Grow Up to be Cowboys"

Now Roxy and Gunther were friends? Yeesh...

@$enorDutton - Forget abt me what RU listening to, beautiful?

Ignoring Dutton's bad grammar and cheap flirtation, I contemplated making something up—fabricating a song that would make me seem cool—but quickly changed my mind. Not only did I have no idea what would ingratiate me to Roxy, I'd spent the greater part of the evening deciding to be real. So I typed the name of the first song on the playlist I'd just made.

@Moves_like_jagga – The Cure: "Pictures of You"

A second after I pressed send on my phone, I pressed the space bar on my Mac—Spotify was open and the playlist was still up. When I saw my reply to Roxy pop up on my phone screen at the same time the bass guitar and wind chimes of the opening bars embraced me in surround sound, I knew I was already fucking gone.

———

ROXY

I chewed my lip and wrang my hands, acutely aware of the time. Zoë's Cayenne would soon tear down the street and a decision had to be made. For the third time in as many days, it seemed that my existence could tilt and tumble from baring my soul, one status update at a time. However withering *that* thought was, my sense of self-preservation was losing the fight.

I had no one to blame but myself for my predicament, of course. I'd thrown out *"What song are you listening to?"* I'd made it seem casual, like it was a fun little question meant for all my friends to answer. But I knew better, and because Jagger Monroe was not stupid, so did he. His response made me wonder just like I did the first time: did we both just happen to love the same deliciously dark emo hits of yesteryear, or was he speaking directly to me?

Dutton kicking the question back to me gave me an unanticipated opportunity: saying what I was listening to would let me show Jagger my hand. My song was chosen, answer written, thumb poised to tap the arrow on my screen, and my pride nowhere to be found. Zoë's car horn prompted me into action. Before I could think too hard about laying myself bare, I pressed send.

@Roxxy_roxxy_roxx - Mazzy Star: "Fade Into You"

He had me so upside-down, I was barely coherent as I walked down the stairs and climbed into Zoë's car. I awoke from my haze to find that she hadn't started driving. We were still in my driveway and she was looking at me expectantly.

"Well?" she exclaimed exasperatedly.

"Well, what?" I asked warily. With her, it could be anything.

"Were you ever going to tell me about your extracurricular activities on Instagram, or were you thinking I'd just piece it together on my own?"

Oh, God. If Zoë had figured it out, maybe everyone else had. *What must people think of me?*

"It's only been a day..." I stammered weakly, crestfallen that I'd been so obvious. "I didn't think—"

"Didn't think what?" she demanded. "Didn't think I could use an hour or two to pick out a cuter profile picture? Didn't think I might think twice before leading him to believe I spend Monday nights at home listening to love songs?"

What?

"Roxy," she whined miserably, "How could you not tell me you and Gunther became friends? Now he can see everything I've ever written on your profile!"

Oh, thank fuck. She was upset about Gunther.

"Do you think he thinks I'm a freak?" Her tone changed on a dime from admonishment to fear as she handed me her one insecurity. "Sometimes he gives me these weird looks, like I creep him out or something..."

"Zoë..." I chided gently, slipping into best friend mode, "Gunther *does not* think you are a freak. You have to know he only friended me to get closer to you. Has it occurred to you that Jagger friending me out of the blue was just a roundabout way for that to happen? Or that Gunther only acts weird because he likes you so much? It's basic kindergarten psychology, sweetie...you're lucky he doesn't drop sand down your shirt and pull your hair."

Her look of bafflement almost made my secondary theory about Jagger's motives—the one I didn't like to think about—sting a little less.

"Oh." She stared through her windshield, toward the doors of my garage, as if she were trying to work something out in her head.

"Besides," I continued, "if anyone's a freak, it's him, the way he won't even talk to you but waits for you every morning before school."

She blushed slightly and we shared a knowing smile that seemed to quell her doubts.

"So, step on it, bitch, or you're gonna miss your welcome party," I said, pulling my sunglasses out of my pocket and putting them on.

She giggled and did just that. I felt slightly guilty for riding her Gunther high to deflect attention from my Jagger situation. But I was glad she was so absorbed in her own problems that she'd started to lay off of mine. I could barely explain what was happening myself, much less explain it to anybody else.

My problem's car wasn't in the school parking lot as we crawled toward Zoë's regular spot, but Gunther was by Declan's Jeep. Gunther sported his usual expression of fear and reverence that surfaced only around Zoë, murmuring his own hopeful "Mornin'" as we passed, and holding the door for us as we walked inside. It would've been cute to watch their dance if Jagger hadn't been MIA.

I spent the morning mustering the confidence to acknowledge him in Civics, you know...just in case he even showed up. I took the long way to class between Math and PE so I could spy through the window next to the third-floor stairs. In a scan of the parking lot below, I located his car, confirming that he'd come to school. In a scan of my Instagram feed, a couple friends had hearted my response, but not Jagger, nor had he replied.

Whatever courage I'd gathered was dampened the second I walked into the room. Something had changed. He seemed... aloof. I felt stupid and naïve when I slid into my chair and deafening silence resumed, nullifying yesterday's hello. I passed the hour wallowing in insecurity, wading through his schizophrenic behavior and drowning in my original doubts. I was dying to bolt, to find some deserted space in the school where I could pull off my game face and lick my wounds.

The second the bell rang, I hastened to leave, stuffing my books in my backpack. I nearly knocked over a few kids in my mad scramble to get out of the room. As I shuffled into the hall, I remembered that Jagger always went left, which was the same direction it made sense for me to go. I didn't want to chance bumping into him, even accidentally. It looked like I'd be taking the long way to my next class. Again.

I turned right, still stung and confused by his behavior, still wishing for a place to sulk and to let myself get a little mad. He had some nerve, being hot and cold like this. My phone buzzed in my pocket, interrupting my thoughts. Probably Zoë texting me. The part of me that could really use a pep talk and a vent wished I'd already come clean. But it wasn't Zoë—it was an Instagram alert. I read my screen in disbelief.

@moves_like_jagga sent you a private message

English Lit be damned, I did go find a hiding place then: a spot behind the gym where no one ever went. Certain that smoke was shooting out of my ears, I knew I was in no condition to go to class. I didn't want anyone to see how unraveled I was by...

"That enigmatic fuck!" I seethed aloud.

Once I reached the space behind the gym, I didn't sit right away. I thumbed in the code to unlock my phone and swiped the alert on the screen, raging internally all the while.

Who the hell does he think he is, avoiding me like the plague and then PMing me?

Does he get some cheap thrill out of luring girls with faux-emo bullshit, just so he can mess with their minds?

Who does stuff like this?!

Once I abandoned futile speculation, I saw the message:

You rushed out of class pretty quickly. I thought you might like this version.

A second message held a Spotify link and the preview picture of an old white guy with a baseball cap. The caption below the image announced that it was a version of *Fade Into You* by someone named J Mascis. I didn't recognize the name. But it didn't escape my notice that Jagger hadn't sent me The Moth and the Flame version, which, in my opinion, was just okay. The hand that didn't hold the phone was balled into a fist and I narrowed my eyes, as if glaring his thumbnail image on my screen would teleport to his consciousness. I'd *wanted* him to acknowledge my song. But, still, I was spitting mad.

Yes, I'd rushed out of Civics. *But only because he'd ignored me.* Why hadn't he just passed me a note telling me to check my phone?

"I hate you, Jagger Monroe," I growled out loud.

Even as I spoke the words the self-preserving part of me knew that I should feel, the larger part of me laughed at the lie.

SIX
LOVE ON THE BRAIN

Must be love on the brain
that's got me feeling this way.
It beats me black and blue
but it f*cks me so good
and I can't get enough.
-Rihanna, *Love on the Brain*

JAGGER

"Yo, Deck," I said distractedly when he answered his cell.

"What up, J-dawg?" he bellowed cheerfully.

The Spice Girls jab was less than twelve hours old, and any other friend would've whined. That was one thing I respected about Declan—he really knew how to take things in stride.

"Can you swing by Gunther's place and take him to school? I'm running late."

"No worries, dude...everything alright?"

"Yeah, man. I just overslept."

I was scrolling through my iTunes library even as I spoke, some blind sense of purpose in control of my actions. I mumbled an absent goodbye to Declan as my eyes continued to scan. There was a version I'd heard once—a solo track by the front man in Dinosaur Jr.—but it was in my other music library and I'd forgotten his name, so I had to look up the song. By the time I stopped to think about what I was doing, I was looking it up on Spotify, saving it to my private playlist, then opening the app on my phone and copying the link to the song. I must've been out of it not to have heard my mom come in.

"Listening to music at...8AM?" she asked with her peaceful voice and a glance at the clock.

"Just uploading my homework," I lied smoothly.

My mom knew I transferred my music comp assignments from my computer to my phone. She thoroughly approved of my high-tech set-up, though it didn't hold a candle to her studio downstairs. Old friends from her industry days sometimes visited, taking inspiration from the nature energy. Some amazing tracks had been recorded, right here in this house.

"Don't forget to eat something..." she scolded lightly from the doorway. "I'd rather you be late than be hungry."

After mousing my desktop into sleep mode and pocketing my phone, I grabbed my backpack and made my way to the door.

"Love you, Mom." I leaned down to kiss her cheek and squeeze her hand as I passed.

My phone burned a hole in my pocket all fucking morning, and when Roxy flashed me a blushing smile as she slid into her seat in Civics, I wasn't sure I could go through with it. Speaking to her right here in front of God and everybody would produce definitive evidence that something had changed. Maybe I'd over-estimated myself—overestimated my *plan*—overestimated my confidence that Civics class was a safe haven where I could say a few words to her without anyone seeing or caring.

Shit.

I spent the entire period overthinking it—so long that I was surprised when the bell rang. She seemed in a hurry to leave. As she stuffed her books into her backpack and shot toward the front of the classroom, I kicked myself mentally. I'd let my moment pass. And what was I supposed to do now? Try again tomorrow? Like, hey "Roxy, remember that song you were listening to on Monday? It's two days later, and even though I lost them yesterday, I found my balls again today. By the way, here's an obscure cover I wanted to share with you." Yes. If I was going to do this, waiting even another minute would make it extra weird. Before I could change my mind, I tapped out a quick message, sent the link and tried to forget about it for awhile.

After school, I headed to my volunteer gig, glad to kill a few hours at the hospital before reprising my stalker role at home. After dinner with my parents and an uncommonly lengthy session with my piano, I ventured upstairs to the bat cave. The grin that arose when my eyes fell to her update was unstoppable. It was an image that only a die-hard music listener would understand. A white play button sat largest in the middle; forward and back controls flanked its side and an icon with crossed arrows on the left denoted shuffle play. The sole splash of green belonged to the icon on the right: curved head-to-tail arrows that combined to form an oval. Roxy was telling me she had the song on repeat.

ROXY

"Earth to Roxy!"

Zoë's muted voice reached me from over the sound of my music at the same time her waving palm entered my vision. I tugged out a white earbud as I thumbed the pause button my phone.

"You are *way* too into your music," Zoë chided lightly, and not for the first time. I muttered an apology and didn't mention that it wasn't my music—it was Jagger's.

Ever the chatterbox, Zoë was content to dive right into the afternoon's news as we walked to the car. The only classes we shared in common were U.S. History in second period and, of course, lunch. Since this was high school, a lot could happen between lunch and the end of the day. I hummed and nodded in all of the appropriate places as we sped down mostly-empty roads. Traffic thinned the farther we got from school. I still hadn't gotten used to certain things about this part of California—gray skies in most other places meant rain. Winters here were overcast, but half the time, it was bone dry.

"Hey..." I remembered as I was getting out of the Cayenne. "Was there a quiz in English Lit?"

"We started *The Catcher in the Rye.* Didn't you go to class?"

"I wasn't feeling well." Technically, it was true.

"Send you my notes?" she offered.

"Thanks anyway," I replied. "I had to read it last year." Actually, it had been twice—once at my old school and again at the new.

The second I got inside, I dropped my backpack like a rock, shot up to my room, and threw my phone onto my speaker dock. I'd heard other versions before, but this one was...unbelievable. I listened to it over and over, each new play soothing my anger with Jagger like a salve.

It was a nice gesture, I told myself now.

He must love this song too, to have a version like this.

Maybe he's an introvert.

How quickly I had changed my tune. I didn't even think about dinner until my dad popped his head in my room. His presence startled me, and I shot upright in embarrassment, as if I had been caught doing something wrong. He'd have known by then that I hadn't cooked. No set table and no smells coming from the kitchen meant nothing to eat.

"The diner?" he asked, raising an eyebrow.

"Yeah." I managed a sheepish smile. He smiled back. My dad was cool.

"Five minutes." He closed my door again on his way out.

I agonized less over updating my status this time, some part of me knowing I had surrendered to playing this out. A little screen shot of my play buttons, a little filter to brighten up the green repeat symbol, and, boom!

I tried to maintain a façade of normalcy as I rode with my dad to the diner. He put on a mellow Iron & Wine. He was quiet like me and we didn't say much when we were together, but he still felt more present than my mom. It still startled me sometimes—someone asking about my day, caring about my grades and telling me I couldn't go out unless my homework was done. Maybe one day the novelty of daily parental supervision would wear off. So far, it hadn't.

"You hear from your mom?"

I shoved half of the longest french fry I could find in my mouth and chewed it very slowly. I'd been avoiding my mother and didn't want to talk about her. She didn't call regularly, but when she really wanted to talk, she'd call me over and over. Lately, she'd been bugging me about plans for her wedding.

"Yeah...I need to call her back," I admitted vaguely. "The time difference makes it kinda hard."

Selfish Bliss was on the European leg of its tour, which made it plausible that my mother's incessant calls would have come in at indecent hours. But my mother didn't keep decent hours. She'd been calling around dinner time for me, which was around three in the morning for her.

"You know what happens when you avoid her..." He gave me a look.

"Yeah, I do know." I picked up another fry. "She calls you. Then both of you get on my case."

When my dad put down his burger and sighed, I felt a twinge of guilt. He was only trying to do the right thing. I'd been around custody agreements long enough to know how her not being able to reach me could be perceived if she reported it to the courts.

"She wants me to come in April." I really didn't want to talk to my dad about the wedding, even though he wasn't in love with her anymore. She'd broken his heart twice: once by leaving him as a man, and again by taking his child. To add insult to injury, she'd left for the sake of a dream that had once belonged to them both.

That was how they'd fallen in love: he wrote songs and she sang—he even knew his way around a guitar. They'd have moved to Nashville to perform as a duo. Then I'd come along. My dad had done what he had to, to support his family. My flighty mother had been impatient, but my practical dad been content to delay. It was the end of their romance—her resenting him for giving up on Nashville. Him resenting her for looking down her nose at the better-than-decent life he could give them by working his trade and staying in Rye.

"April, as in, Spring Break?" My dad snaked one of my fries and dipped it in way too much ketchup.

I didn't know why I kept stalling. He would find out either way. "April, as in, pull me out of school for a week so I can go to Mexico for the wedding. She's been bugging me to get a passport and to convince you to sign the release."

My dad stopped chewing. I winced. This recalled the most vicious fight between them—the incident that made it so they couldn't even stay friends. When my mother had left him, she hadn't negotiated him seeing me—she'd packed our things and taken me to Nashville with her. And she'd left like a thief in the night. It had been illegal for her to take me, without his permission, across state lines. He'd never forgiven her for leaving like she did and essentially kidnapping me in the process.

"I'm not gonna stop you from going to your mother's wedding."

"I shouldn't miss school," I hedged.

He opened a napkin, wiped his mouth, and fixed me with another look. "I'll write you a note."

"I don't want to go." I hated that it came out as a whisper due to the sudden lump in my throat.

He looked at me hard—that sweeping kind of look that studied every inch of my face—with tawny eyes that were identical to mine.

"She's still your mother."

"I know."

"Something about Adam make you nervous?"

I shook my head quickly. "It's not that." Nothing made my dad go all papa bear faster than thinking about whether it was safe to be around my mom's men. There had been a lot of them over the years. Adam was an okay guy, but it was still my mom's same scene: her partying like she was twenty-five instead of thirty-five; her treating me like I was twenty instead of seventeen; her performing for everyone—acting as if we were more like sisters or best friends than mother and daughter.

"I'll just be an accessory," I finally admitted.

My dad pursed his lips and gave me a sorrowful look. For a minute, I thought he'd say what it looked like he wanted to. Instead, he asked for the check. Outside, he gave me one of the kinds of hugs he'd been giving me since I was a kid and put on David Bowie when we got into the car.

I was proud of myself for staving off the impulse to check my Instagram feed as his truck hummed smoothly over empty, tree-lined roads. But I wasn't strong enough not to check the second I got back in my room. I smiled when I read a post from Gunther that had been hearted by *Zoë*. That had to mean that they'd become Instagram friends. I didn't bother with the rest of my feed.

Tonight I was anxious. Impatient. Relentlessly focused on Jagger. Resolved to stop for nothing else until I found his update. This one was an image that simply said "cover songs" and he'd written a question in the caption space.

@Moves_like_jagga: What cover song is better than the original?

Diligently avoiding thoughts of ponytails being tugged and sand down shirts and advice I'd given Zoë about how strangely boys acted when they liked you, I typed in the name of my favorite cover.

SEVEN

HALLELUJAH

But remember when I moved in you,
and the holy dove was moving too,
and every breath we drew was Hallelujah.
-Jeff Buckley, *Hallelujah*
(Originally written/performed by Leonard
     Cohen)

JAGGER

My parents looked rightfully suspicious when I practically skipped into the kitchen later that night, the polar opposite of their resigned, fretful son who had barely choked down dinner an hour before. I hummed lightly as I helped myself to a bounty of strawberry ice cream with crumbled Golden Grahams on top, too elated over Roxy's reaction to find the will to care. I kissed my mom on the cheek, squeezed my dad's shoulder, chirruped a goodnight and (I'm ashamed to admit) flitted upstairs.

I was maniacally thrilled by her status update. Roxy had it on repeat. And, somehow, I *just knew* she did. I pictured what her bedroom in her split-level house must be like, imagined what expression would be on her face and what thoughts in her mind as she listened to a song that had possessed me dozens of times before. I put the song on again myself after I read her post, sprawling out on my bed and staring at the ceiling, wondering whether listening to the same song at the same time made us cosmically joined. When I closed my eyes, I pictured her next to me, our fingers intertwined as we found each other in the music.

Music was the one thing that I had ever really cared about, that I had never defiled with pretense or front. I protected the musical parts of my life jealously. I'd known how to read music before I'd known how to read the alphabet. Every music requirement I'd taken since the sixth grade had been an independent study. I'd gone to some of the country's most prestigious summer conservatories. And I went to a ton of shows—from classical to metal—with my parents or by myself.

And Roxy...she wasn't listening to whatever the radio was playing—not drinking whatever musical Kool Aid the industry was telling kids to like. I'd seen her with her little iPod Nano—noticed it even before we became on friends on Instagram. What I wouldn't give to browse her music library. No woman had ever tried to relate to me on this level, much less understood it was the only language I really spoke. Yet, she did. And she wanted to speak it with me. Needing to feel close to her, I tapped to wake up my phone. Time had passed since I'd posted my question about covers. I could see already that the reply list was long.

@LaurenHalloran$ – Lissie's cover of Lady Gaga: "Bad Romance"

I scoffed. Like hell it was.

@Tessa$tack – Jimmy Fallon's cover of "Whip My Hair"

Yeah. I wasn't going to gratify that with a response.

@DeckDeckGoo$e – The original is always better.

Et tu, Declan? Not only did nobody I know seem to have any taste in music—after three responses and no Roxy I was starting to get antsy. Thankfully, Gunther replied to Deck.

@CivilWarBuff$ – Always @DeckDeckGoo$e? Three words, son: Johnny Cash—"Hurt"

Finally, a good cover, I thought in relief.

@OhAnnika$ – Gunther's right—what about The Clash doing "I Fought the Law"?

@DeckDeckGoo$e – You gotta do better than that, babe.

@OhAnnika$ – Concrete Blonde: "Everybody Knows"

I liked the Leonard Cohen version better, but I kept my mouth shut. Declan needed to be schooled.

@A$eVentura – Marilyn Manson's "Sweet Dreams"

@DeckDeckGoo$e – You scare me, @A$eVentura

I snorted around a mouthful of ice cream.

@Roxxy_roxxy_roxx – Jeff Buckley – "Hallelujah"

I stopped breathing—and not just because Roxy had answered—because Jeff Buckley was *my favorite fucking artist,* and that song was *made* for him.

@DeckDeckGoo$e – @Roxxy_roxxy_roxx Touché

Still floored, I opened my chat window and fired off an impulsive message.

@moves_like_jagga: Fucking fantastic song.

I second-guessed myself the moment I pressed send and for the long three minutes that passed before I got a response. Instead of calming when I heard the little chime that signaled her answer, my heart beat faster.

@Roxxy_roxxy_roxx: Out of all the people who have covered it, JB's is the best, IMO

I hadn't thought past my opening line, and spent a panicked moment reaching for something intelligent to say. She surprised me by continuing straightaway, as if chatting with me were the easiest thing in the world.

@Roxxy_roxxy_roxx: I always wondered, though, why he left out LC's last two verses. They really change the meaning of the song...

Not only did she have taste—this girl knew her music. I fought the urge to pepper her with all the questions that had been plaguing my mind.

@moves_like_jagga: I'll bet the studio execs made him shorten it. Maybe you could find a concert version where he goes all out?

@Roxxy_roxxy_roxx: Trust me. I've tried. And thanks for the J Mascis—it's a great recording.

BeCoolBeCoolBeCoolBeCool

@moves_like_jagga: My pleasure

There was a lull in the conversation and I scolded myself again to *think, damn it!*

@Roxxy_roxxy_roxx: So, I guess I'll see you in class tomorrow?

I wilted a little. *Too slow.*

@moves_like_jagga: Sure thing

I had "Good night, Roxy" typed and ready to go when her next message came up.

@Roxxy_roxxy_roxx: Maybe then you'll tell me your favorite cover...I'm not the only one with good taste in music

My face flushed deeply at the compliment and I imagined I looked like her for a moment, though not nearly as cute.

@moves_like_jagga: Maybe...

I bit my lip against a shit-eating grin.

@moves_like_jagga: Good night, Roxy

@Roxxy_roxxy_roxx: Good night, Jagger

———

ROXY

My face tilted skyward and a smile found my lips as the sun

kissed my starved shoulders. The rarely-used quad was buzzing with students enjoying the same thing as me. I had chosen a picnic table off to the side, and was listening to a playlist. I'd shed my hoodie and put on my sunglasses. Shy girl Roxy was nowhere to be found when something like sun was at stake. Ignoring the chill in the air, I kept myself warm with Air's *Sexy Boy*, the best finds I'd ever gotten from my Aunt Keri. It was a rare recording I'd ripped off of a CD ages ago. Nothing on this playlist was released on the streaming services, so I had to listen on my old Nano.

Everything was bliss until a shadow crossed my path and my music abruptly stopped.

"Motherf—" I started to mutter.

I opened my eyes to see the retreating form of none other than Jag Monroe. When I caught a faint waft of his scent, my eyelids fluttered. Remembering myself, I glanced down at the table, and gaped at what I saw. My Nano had been stealthily replaced by a little green iPod. Somehow, he'd managed to disconnect my player and attach my earphones to his, all before I could even open my eyes. I snapped my gaze back up towards him and I leveled what I hope came off as a glare. He now leaned with his back against a far wall, one knee bent and foot bracing the brick as he palmed my Nano, too busy smirking to notice my scowl as he shuffled through what I sincerely hoped was only my music.

That infuriating, brilliant bastard!

I picked up the iPod and hit Play, then resumed my prior stance with as much disinterest as possible. I couldn't let him see how he unraveled me, how ravenous I was for anything he gave. A familiar folk guitar that I couldn't immediately place eased me into a song I didn't quite recognize but somehow remembered I loved.

Busted flat in Baton Rouge,
waitin' for a train and I's feelin'
near as faded as my jeans...

Jagger's favorite cover song was the Janis Joplin version of
"Me and Bobby McGee"? The same Janis Joplin whose bluesy
voice had crooned intensely to me despite ancient speakers and
the scratches and flaws in Renee's old vinyl? I was the one who
had begged her to get rid of it—to step into the 21st century and
buy bluetooth speakers for the living room. I thought of Jefferson
Airplane, and Tom Petty, and all the other bands I'd missed out
on since we packed away our old LPs.

Damn, I forgot how good this song was...

I resisted the urge to open my mouth and sing along, settling
instead for humming softly. I figured he'd given me just one, like
last time, but things became clear when there was a second, then
a third, then a fourth. Joe Cocker's version of *A Little Help from
My Friends,* The Sundays' version of *Wild Horses,* Iron & Wine's
version of *Such Great Heights*...and they weren't all studio
versions, either. Something sublime took hold as I listened, face
upturned, eyes still closed, basking in the warmth of the sun. I'd
never heard Tori Amos sing *Daniel* or Ann and Nancy Wilson
sing *The Battle of Evermore,* and he had a cut of The Indigo Girls
doing *Mona Lisas and Mad Hatters* that was just...amazing.

This wasn't Jagger throwing me tiny little morsels—this was...
alright, I didn't know what it was. But he'd stolen my Nano and
made me a fucking *playlist.* And not just any playlist—a playlist
that had, like, ten emo songs on it. What's more, I'd let him. This
was definitely big.

I spent the rest of lunch in the same position, listening
through the songs he gave me. The bell rang at the same time my
stomach growled and I realized I'd daydreamed straight through

lunch. Before I could come up with a plan for how to shove down enough food to avoid embarrassing myself in Civics, I saw something that hadn't been there before. On top of my books sat a perfect red apple. I think we both know who left it.

EIGHT

THE WAY

They made up their minds
and they started packing.
They left before the sun came up that day.
An exit to eternal summer slacking.
But where were they going
without ever knowing the way?
-Fastball, *The Way*

JAGGER

I grabbed the plate of cookies as I swept into the house, startling my mother as I tore up the steps, barely stopping to give her a kiss. Once in my room, I kicked off my shoes and flopped down on my bed. I blew my hair out of my eyes as I reached into my pockets, eager for a thorough exploration of Roxy's Nano.

I smiled at the memory of her flummoxed expression in Civics as she'd asked for her iPod back. I'd just kept my eyes forward and smiled as I slowly shook my head "no". She'd muttered a soft "asshole" under her breath, but I'd spied a tiny smile. I pretended not to notice how she reached out to worry the little green Shuffle between her fingers several times during the class.

Scrolling through her music list at leisure now, I fell more than a little in love. Her collection had some of everything—from Pentatonix to Parliament, from Queen to Queensryche, from The Supremes to Sublime, from Beethoven to the Buena Vista Social Club. She had one hit wonders, and soundtracks, and bands I didn't recognize, but the few unfamiliar songs I listened to, I liked. She had the cutest little names for her playlists, things like "Groggy" and "Aggro" and "Low". Best of all was her "Top 25 Most Played" list, which was full of songs I fucking loved.

This girl is perfect.

The thought infiltrated my being, the chant of the mantra chipping away at my resolve with each repetition. Yet as intense as this *thing* was, we remained oddly estranged. I had to do something about that.

I went to my computer and opened up iTunes, determined to add some stuff she didn't have to her Nano. It was only six o'clocked, a little earlier than I wanted to start what was quickly becoming my nightly Instagram feast, but I was obsessed, so I logged on anyway.

The first thing I saw was a friend request from Zoë DuBois. I hit "confirm" immediately. That had only been a matter of time. Her feed revealed an eclectic mix of posts about everything from fashion, to art, to roller derby. A quick scan through revealed that Gunther had hearted them all. Gunther rarely posted anything. I had to talk to that kid. Now that he was getting somewhere with Zoë, he had to step up his game.

Declan's feed, as usual, was full of selfies of he and Annika. Annika's feed was always full of classic cars. The ones they worked on at her brothers' garage were pretty sweet. I would've normally stopped to scan through what was new and look back at some of my favorites. But, today I was on a mission: cyber-flirt with Roxy. I arrived at her feed to find a stop-motion image of a scene with legos: a lego kid with spiky brown hair and an outraged expression chasing a lego storm trooper who was running away. The storm trooper had a teddy bear in his hand and was looking back at the lego kid who was chasing him. The caption read: *I'd better get it back tomorrow.*

I chuckled out loud, and for the second time in as many days, sent her an impulse chat:

@moves_like_jagga: Or what?

This time, she hit me right back.

@Roxxy_roxxy_roxx: Or you'll find out just how L.A. I am.

I snorted.

@moves_like_jagga: I bring you music and an apple and you repay me with threats?

Shit. I was grinning again.

@Roxxy_roxxy_roxx: The apple was the least you could do.

@Roxxy_roxxy_roxx: What do you want with my iPod, anyway?

It's a key puzzle piece in my obsession to know everything about you.

Yeah. That one I didn't type out.

@moves_like_jagga: It's collateral while you hold onto mine.

Yeah. What I actually wrote was a lot less creepy.

@Roxxy_roxxy_roxx: The Shuffle isn't even your real iPod— maybe you ought to let me hold on to that black Nano of yours

The thought was mildly terrifying. Showing her my iPod would mean showing her...everything.

@moves_like_jagga: Ha! Fat chance, Vega.

I ignored the significance of just having put her on a last-name basis.

@Roxxy_roxxy_roxx: Just watch your left pocket—that's all I'm saying...

I tried to quell the strange combination of lust and realization. Her talk about holding my Nano and reaching into my pocket to grab my iPod was causing my body to react. Something else was significant: she wouldn't have known the color of my iPod or my habit of keeping it in my left pocket unless she'd paid attention. How long had Roxy been paying attention to me?

@moves_like_jagga: Did you like the songs, at least?

From the look on her face, it seemed like she had. That vision would stay with me for awhile: Roxy sitting on top of that picnic table, shoulders bare, face upturned toward the sun. Every day it became clearer: she and I had a lot more in common than I'd ever stopped to consider.

@Roxxy_roxxy_roxx: They were all great...but you still haven't answered my question: which one is your favorite?

I had to know what she thought of me, which was why I told her to...

@moves_like_jagga: Guess

@Roxxy_roxxy_roxx: (rolls eyes) Or, you could tell me...

I really liked this version of her.

@moves_like_jagga: Best song is "Hallelujah" but best improvement on the original is "Mad World"

@Roxxy_roxxy_roxx: ::nods approvingly::

I fucking laughed. We spent what felt like just a few minutes but what I later realized had been an hour chatting about other covers, and other bands, we liked. I realized I'd been stalling on dinner for longer than I thought when I heard my dad's footsteps outside my room.

@moves_like_jagga: Uh-oh. Dinnertime.

@Roxxy_roxxy_roxx: Fuck—I just looked at the clock! I need to get to dinner, too.

With little time left, I grasped for parting words that would make me seem cool.

I can't remember the last time I enjoyed talking to someone so much, Roxy.

I'm really starting to like you, *like you.*
I'm kind of fucked up, but you make me want to be better.
So, what do you say...will you go out with me some time?
@moves_like_jagga: Good night, Vega
@Roxxy_roxxy_roxx: Next time, Monroe
Tomorrow, I was going to talk to that girl.

NINE

HOT AND COLD

You overthink,
always speak cryptically.
I should know
that you're no good for me.
-Katy Perry, *Hot n Cold*

ROXY

I tried not to blush at Jagger's slight bow as he opened the door for me the next morning. Zoë and Gunther were flirting obscenely as the four of us walked into school. Unsurprisingly, Jag didn't actually speak, which was probably just as well. His hair was still damp and his scent was strong. His aroma held no notes of the Axe body wash most of the other boys used—Jagger smelled ten times better, like tobacco and cedar. When I realized how freshly bathed he was, thoughts of water on his skin and the things that teenage boys do in the shower pretty much rendered me speechless. It was a short walk to homeroom, which only Zoë and I had together, and the four of us stopped at the door.

"See you later, Zoë," Gunther drawled in a hush.

"Bye, Gunther," Zoë smiled coquettishly.

Gunther grinned like an idiot. I turned to Jagger, expecting he'd be enjoying the show, but he was laser-focused on me. *I have plans for you*, his green eyes seemed to say, as a smirk played across his lips. It was the first time he'd ever regarded me directly. Its intensity tilted my world.

I wandered, dazed, into the room, and sank into my seat. I heard nothing—not roll call, not announcements, not the bell. I came to at Zoë's nudge.

"Meet me at the usual place?"

I had no idea what she was talking about.

"*For the pep rally*, Roxx—weren't you listening?"

This, from a woman for whom, minutes before, nothing outside of Gunther had existed.

"Uh, when is it?" I managed, pushing a stray lock of hair behind my ear.

"Right after lunch—they've cancelled sixth and seventh."

I wanted to whine like a petulant child: "*But sixth period is my class with Jagger!*" Instead, I nodded at Zoë and we agreed to meet near the trophy case outside of the gym.

By 9AM, I was still annoyed that I would not be seeing Jagger. By 10AM, I was feeding an ornate fantasy of him kidnapping me from the pep rally, of us lying close on the football field and listening to his iPod from the same set of little white earbuds. By 11AM, I was chiding myself for having *ornate fantasies* about Jagger Monroe in so undignified a class as Trig. When, by lunch, my vision had morphed into us dry humping on said football field, I snapped myself guiltily out of fantasizing about him at all.

I'd been in Rye for six solid months without hooking up with a single person. Just because no one in Rye was my type didn't mean I wasn't still a red-blooded American girl. In L.A., I'd gone the friends with benefits route with my neighbor, Jason. But here, I had no friends to have benefits with. It didn't help that Jagger was sex incarnate, and was suddenly being nicer to me. It was easier to keep it in check when he'd been a complete asshole, but was it any wonder I lusted after him now?

Take a number, Vega, some insidious voice taunted.

My eyes slid across the cafeteria to where Lauren Halloran sat. I'd always been embarrassed about her desperate plays at Jagger—and when I say "embarrassed", I mean embarrassed for her. Apparently they'd dated. He wasn't a jerk to her or anything, but she was the only one who didn't see how disinterested he was. I could admit that I'd judged her harshly, branding her as foolish and insecure and weak.

But what about me?

Because wasn't it me who pursued him now? And wouldn't it be the watchful eyes of my classmates who might soon judge me? It occurred to me then that trifling with Jagger could turn me into Lauren Halloran—if I didn't get a fucking grip.

Had he seduced her with mix tapes? I wondered, unclear on the details of their relationship and not even sure it had been a relationship at all. Whatever had happened had happened last year, before I came, and I was still too secretive about whatever this was to just ask Zoë for the backstory. Before I could speculate on how Lauren had gotten so obsessed with Jag, a flash of his tousled hair invaded my vision. My traitorous lips curled up in a smile...until I saw who he was with.

Ex-hookup number two was Jamie Victor, and her advances were bolder than Lauren's. She'd draped her hand on his shoulder, with her forearm down his back, and she leaned in to whisper in his ear. Their backs were to me, so I couldn't see his face, but I noted how he didn't brush her off. God help me, but I was suddenly seething with anger at everything—at her, at him, at myself.

Was this my fate? To become one of his harem? His friend list on Instagram confirmed a sizeable herd.

You cannot fall for Jagger Monroe, I admonished myself with forced resolve.

So we'd bantered on Instagram and liked a few of the same songs. So he made me a playlist—he was probably just bored.

More like on the hunt for his next victim.

At that, I flew out of my lunchroom chair before Zoë—or anybody—could find me. I did go lie in the football field then, all by myself, with the little green iPod in tow. The polar opposite of the day before, I stared, open-eyed at the sky. I was sprawled out and laid open and futilely hopeful that something would give me a sign. My instincts told me there was something special about him, that he wouldn't hurt me, that I made him drop his defenses. But he wasn't really letting me see him, either. He just kept pushing towards me, and I had no explanation as to why.

By the time I met Zoë to head into the gym, I was as clueless as before. Ten minutes after taking my seat on the bleachers, my mood became foul. My voice of reason had beat the hell out of my hopeful delusions. My lack of sustenance left me irritable and weak. Zoë's radiating bliss as she texted with Gunther only reminded me of what I didn't have. And the last thing I needed was pep.

I did the only thing that could distract me from this torture. I pulled out my cell and got on Instagram, not for *his* benefit for once—so that other friends and other places would commiserate with me. I posted a "Keep Calm and Eat Tacos" meme I liked. It was meant for my old crew. God, did I miss the tacos in L.A.

@Roxxy_roxxy_roxx: I'd take down a nun for a taco from La Pancha. I'd settle for something with caffeine and sugar.

I fired it off irritably and immediately, before going back to my feed and scrolling in a very un-merry way. I tried not to dwell on it as an act of defiance—as proof that not everything was about him. When a teacher glared at me for having my phone out, I slammed it back into my pocket. I hadn't refocused on Coach

Bradley's lousy job of emceeing for two minutes when I heard the hushed whisper of my name.

"Roxy Vega," the unfamiliar female voice whisper-urged, "She's, like, two rows behind you."

I had no clue what was going on. Looking down the bleachers to the sea of kids seated in front of me, it seemed that some kind of wave was passing through the crowd.

"Roxy Vega," an unfamiliar, bored-sounding voice instructed, and the strange movements of the crowd continued.

By then, even Zoë had caught on and she fixed me in a glance of confusion just as two items were dropped onto my lap. Reflexively, I snatched up a red Coke can, then I noticed the bag of Skittles. I scanned the crowd then, at last permitting myself to look for him. He smirked when he saw me before turning his attention to something in his palm.

His phone.

I set aside my snacks to look at mine. With I opened Instagram to find a screen shot from an old Skittles commercial, my hopeful delusions returned.

@moves_like_jagga: Taste the rainbow.

TEN

IRIS

And I'd give up forever to touch you
'cause I know that you feel me somehow.
You're the closest to heaven that I'll ever be
and I don't want to go home right now.
-Goo Goo Dolls, *Iris*

JAGGER

"Hey there, little man..." I whispered to baby Nick, a wide smile spreading across my face.

He wasn't old enough to smile yet or move around much, but his eyes were open and he looked much healthier than he had when he was born. It was after school and I was at the hospital starting my volunteer gig shift. Almost no one knew that, on Tuesdays and Thursdays, I cuddled newborn babies who were stuck in the ICU.

Some of the babies had to be there for weeks. It was really hard on the parents. Even if the moms were on maternity leave, sometimes they had other kids to take care of at home and most of the dads had jobs. The hospital arranged a small army of cuddlers to step in. The science said that babies needed the contact to develop essential social bonding hormones and interaction skills. All common sense and decency said that babies—especially ones away from their families—needed to be loved and held. So, twice a week, I layered in linens provided by the parents so that the babies would associate being nurtured with the scent of their own homes.

Not just anyone could be a cuddler, of course—they had to screen for baby-stealing lunatics. And beyond all the rigorous criminal and background checks, cuddlers had to be good with babies. Another thing that wasn't widely known: the nurses called me "The Baby Whisperer" for my talent to calm babies with my voice. But I was driven by more than altruism. Being here was cathartic.

"He's happy to see you." A nurse named Grace smiled kindly, glancing at us briefly as she swaddled a baby close by.

"I'm happy to see him." I smiled back, before lifting the little bundle to settle him in my arms.

I had a brother once. Anthony was his name. He'd lived for seven weeks. I'd visited him every day of his life in this very room, but I'd loved him before he was born. They say babies connect with music and voices even within the womb. When my mom was pregnant with him, my dad and I would talk to her belly and take turns playing him CDs. I'd sit with my mom on the piano bench when he was restless and she would play him soothing concertos. I would play him *Hot Cross Buns*. She told me stories of when she'd carried me and how happy they'd been that I was coming, how they'd done the same things for me.

He was born prematurely and through a difficult labor. Not all of his organs functioned properly and he was weak. Since he couldn't come home, we'd visit him here. Given my dad's position at the hospital, they made sure I cleaned up and wore scrubs and looked the other way on the "no children in NICU" rule. What they said about babies being able to hear in utero must have been true. He, too, had calmed at the sound of my voice. Most days he was too weak to be held, but I remember each time that I did. People who thought six years old was too young of an age to remember something like that were dead fucking wrong. I remembered every moment with him.

When he died, it decimated my world, pulling all of us into a darkness I don't think any of us completely survived. My dad took a hiatus from medicine. My mom barely spoke for weeks. They sent me to live with my cousins in Chicago that summer. I came home that fall to altered parents: a mother so paranoid over my safety that she smothered me with her protection; a father too grief-stricken to face his family, who started spending all his time at work.

Things were better now. It was hard to believe it had been ten years. But, to arrive here I'd learned how to cope. During the bad years, music drowned out the sounds of my parents fighting. During the sad years, it filled the silence. When I went to dark places, it joined me. At times, it gave me hope, and in its words, it held the promise of a life much different from this.

Nick's tiny cry broke me out of my thoughts. I often thought deep in this place. Stopping my slow pacing, I sat us in a rocker and hummed my own little lullaby. When he calmed, I stroked his tiny cheek and hugged him a little closer. When his eyes fell shut and his breathing evened, I returned to my own thoughts. Like wondering what must have happened to Roxy to make her listen to the music she did.

"How's he doing?"

This time it was my father's voice that broke me away from my thoughts. He often visited me here. "I had a free minute and thought I'd come by," he always said, though I knew he was busy and made time to come.

"Much better," I said, smiling up at my dad, showing him I

was okay. He still worried, sometimes, that I'd never be whole. In that, I think he was right.

"How are *you* doing?" he asked in the voice of a father, not a doctor.

I met a girl. She's beautiful, and she has passion and depth. I like her so much it scares me, but fuck it. She's worth laying it on the line. I had grand plans to talk to her today, but got cockblocked by a lame-ass pep rally and I had to leave right after school to come here. Maybe I'll chat with her tonight on Instagram—I've become quite the cyber-stalker.

"Really good, Dad," I said honestly, and he beamed.

We sat in companionable silence for a bit, as was our normal routine. Each time, I would offer to let him hold the baby for awhile and each time, he sadly refused. Noticing the time, he got up to return to his shift and we said we'd see each other at home.

"By the way...stop down to see Dr. Sturman before you leave. She has something she thinks you may want."

I raised my eyebrow at my dad's cryptic smile. His chuckle followed him down the hall.

ELEVEN
I CAN'T WAIT

My love, tell me what it's all about.
You've got something
that I can't live without.
Happiness is so hard to find.
Hey baby, tell me what is on your mind.
-Nu Shooz, *I Can't Wait*

ROXY

In place of a peaceful afternoon spent obsessing over Jagger, I fell prey to Zoë's third degree. At the assembly, she'd swiftly ditched her texting with Gunther, demanding to know who sent me food and why. I wasn't about to get into it in a crowded gymnasium so instead of answering, I'd poured half of my Skittles in her hand. When I saw her in the parking lot at the end of eighth period, she shoved her phone in my face.

"Taste the rainbow?" she whisper-hissed with shocked accusation.

"Since when are you friends with Jagger?" I hedged indignantly.

"Since *get in the fucking car!*" she ordered, knowing we couldn't speak of this here.

We zipped out of the parking lot at unauthorized speeds, turning not towards my house but toward hers. I scrolled through my phone, predictably obsessed with whether Jagger had updated again. He hadn't, but the selfie I found of Zoë and Gunther, both of them starry-eyed and his arms around her was big news. But the caption was bigger.

@DerbyGirlZoe: Status change: in a relationship

I pulled the same move she'd just done to me: leveling an accusing glance as I showed her my screen.

"Looks like we have some catching up to do," she conceded with an eyebrow arch.

When we got back to her place, her housekeeper had made us a snack. Since Zoë was practically an adult, nobody ever called Niede a nanny, but for how often Zoë's parents were away, Niede was the most consistent adult in Zoë's life. It made me more than a little uncomfortable—not that her parents left her alone, but that they'd outsourced her care to hired help. I didn't know what was worse—a mother who didn't stop long enough to think about why leaving your kid alone so often was wrong, or a mom who did think about it and fixed it with money.

But I couldn't think about that now. I was starving for real nourishment. Over chicken salad on whole wheat, I gave Zoë an abridged version of the Jagger story. I told her we'd chatted briefly about music, that he'd made a few recommendations, that we'd only had contact twice. I wasn't lying when I said we'd never talked face to face, but I left out the parts about his playlists. I was still too insecure about his motives to come completely clean.

There was something else: yes, she was my best friend, but she had a vested interest in me and Jagger becoming a couple. I wondered how much her crazy prediction that Jagger had a crush on me was about what she actually saw vs. what she read too far into and hoped could one day be true.

"Stop grilling me about Jagger!" I exclaimed gently at some point "It's your turn to spill about Gunther."

Cartoon hearts and blue-jays orbited her head when I dropped the G-word. By the time she finished telling me about their budding romance, about him walking her to class and calling her every night, the comparative evidence—that nothing of consequence was going on between Jagger and me —was ample.

When I returned home that evening, I had made a decision of survival. I knew that I had to back off. I waited until late to log onto Instagram. I hoped that after seeing the image I posted of a cupcake with a skull and crossbones on it would make him get the point.

@Roxxy_roxxy_roxx: Crashing from my sugar high...

After typing my message, and texting an excuse to Zoë about driving myself to school the next day, I turned off my phone.

I rolled into school the next morning deliberately late. I told my dad I had period cramps, so he wrote me a note. I had a plan for Civics: I'd be cordial, but not hopeful. My days of trying to reach Jagger were over. If he wanted something more than a bizarre, shallow, felonious friendship, he'd have to step up and make his move.

When I reached my seat, my Nano sat on my side of the desk and an unfamiliar set of fancy-looking white earphones were wrapped around the middle of each side before fanning into an elegant bow.

"New headphones?" I asked, fully expecting the question to be rhetorical.

He shrugged and pulled out my chair for me.

"Those are better."

I nearly fell into my proffered seat.

"He speaks!" It was meant sarcastically, but laced with genuine surprise.

His chuckle was drowned out by Mr. McAbee as he started his lesson. I reached into my pocket and pulled out his green Shuffle, sliding it across the table to him. He began scribbling on a piece of paper and clandestinely slid me a note.

I took the liberty of adding some songs to your Nano. I hope you like them.

Thanks, I wrote back. I didn't mean to be terse, but this whole thing was fucking me up and I had to stick to my plan.

What are you up to this weekend? he wrote back a few minutes later.

So now he wanted to be pals? Our need to be stealthy as we passed notes back and forth gave me a minute to form my response.

The usual—polishing the silver, planning my world domination strategy.

When he laughed at that, I bit back a smile.

I got two passes to see Foo Fighters on Sunday, he wrote back.

My eyebrows raised to my hairline when I read the note. Dedicated fan that I am, I knew all about the sold-out charity event they were doing at a small venue in Ft. Bragg. I wanted to be angry that Jagger could afford tickets and I couldn't, but mostly I was just jealous that he would get to see them play.

You'll have to tell me about it, I wrote back trying to keep from looking sad.

I could feel him looking at me then, could feel the warmth radiating off of his skin. That animal magnetism of his was working the hell out of me, and I knew if I looked back at him I'd be a goner. He wrote his next note more slowly and passed it carefully, almost apprehensively. I was almost afraid to read it.

Either that, or you could come with me.

I read it twice. Three times.

Either. That. Or. You. Could. Come. With. Me.

By the time I allowed myself to entertain the thought that Jagger Monroe might be asking me out, he had snatched the paper back and hastily scribbled another message.

I know you like them. You have everything they've ever released on your iPod.

Holy fuck, he *was* really trying to get me to go with him!

It depends, I wrote back, needing to hold on to some shred of my dignity. Things could not progress as they had before.

On what? He shot back. His look of worry didn't escape me. Good.

My mind was *so* made up already—it wasn't like I was going to miss out on Dave Grohl—but Jagger didn't need to know that.

On whether you'll talk to me like I'm a normal person. I'm not texting you all night.

Though he let out a velvet chuckle, I was not laughing. Nor was Mr. McAbee, who leveled his second glare.

Of course we'll talk!

I gestured at the note sarcastically, and fired back:

You just *wrote me a note* to promise we'll talk?

He rolled his eyes as he started writing again.

It would be inappropriate to talk during class, Roxy.

I raised my eyebrow.

More or less appropriate than passing notes?

He chuckled again, quieter this time. Hell if I didn't love the sound.

I'll take your untraditional show of gratitude as a yes. May I pick you up at 5?

I fixed my eyes on the blackboard as I nodded my acquiescence, hating myself for how *fucking easy* he made me. I spent the rest of class so wrapped up in thinking about Sunday that I barely noticed when the bell rang. Before I could rise to stand, he leaned close to whisper in my ear.

"And, Roxy? For the record, you're much better than normal."

By the time I registered the caress of his breath on my neck and the goosebumps that had spread to my fingertips, he was already gone.

PART TWO
EVERLONG

TWELVE
IN A LITTLE WHILE

In a little while,
surely you'll be mine.
In a little while, I'll be there.
In a little while,
this hurt will hurt no more.
I'll be home, love.
-U2, *In a Little While*

JAGGER

Roxy's front door flew open before I made it up the steps of her split-level cabin-style house. It was well-maintained, but typical of the older construction in Rye. Her cheeks were alive with that gorgeous flush and her hair was slightly wild. Only the panicked expression and nervous lip-biting were enough to temporarily distract me from what she wore: her tight blue jeans and little black Foo Fighters hoodie were simple, but utterly distracting. Still, I checked myself, knowing her dad was around.

"I'll explain later, just...*sorry*," she whispered with genuine distress as she ushered me inside.

I'd driven twenty miles an hour slower than my normal speed to get there, and not just to compensate for having left my house so early. It was the first time I was taking a girl on an honest-to-goodness date and I needed the time to rehearse what I'd say to her father.

In my vision, things would go like they did in the movies: Mr. Vega would greet me at the door and cast a disdainfully appraising look before waving me inside. Roxy, of course, would still be upstairs doing whatever girls do while their dates are scrutinized by protective fathers. He'd test my handshake and my eye contact to size up just what kind of boy I was. And, seconds before she floated into earshot, he'd growl a threat that if I laid a hand on his daughter he'd cut off my fucking balls. And who could blame a dad like that? After all, he'd been young once. He knew the hearts of teenage boys.

But Roxy was the one girl I knew I would never want to hurt. My job was to make sure the Mr. Vega knew it too. And because my own dad had long-since prepared me for exactly this sort of situation, I followed Roxy into the living room and looked Mr. Vega straight in the eye.

"Hello, Mr. Vega—I'm Jagger Monroe. It's a pleasure to meet you, sir."

He shook my hand hard, but I gave as good as I got.

"Jagger! Pleasure to finally meet you," he said jovially before withdrawing his hand.

The act of sitting back down in the seat from which he'd stood drew my attention to the startling array of hunting knives that lay before him on the table. I moved instinctively to stand behind a dining room chair, one with a high back that shielded my privates.

"Thank you for allowing Roxy to accompany me to the concert on such short notice. It's a charity show at The Vermillion Room. I'm sure we'll be quite safe."

He resumed sharpening a rather long knife, sporting an eerily cheerful smile as he took his time to answer. By then Roxy had stepped behind him and was mouthing another *'I'm so sorry...'*

"Well, my girl knows how to take care of herself. Don't you, Roxx?" he asked as he picked up a blood orange that he began to peel with the knife. He started at the navel and sliced perfectly roundly and lengthwise to the stem. With shocking speed, he completed the job with minimal strokes, exposing the juicy gloss of a deeply-skinned fruit.

"And I know Jagger will take great care of you...", he looked at me then, the same pleasant smile on his face, "...won't you, son?"

You're creeping me out, Mr. Vega.

I shifted my eyes to Roxy for a second. She looked pretty pissed.

"Concert starts at eight, dad—I'll be home by one," she ground out with thinly-veiled exasperation.

He sliced into the orange with two long, precise cuts, loosening a single section that he quickly ate off of the knife.

"Don't be late, kid," he lightly answered Roxy, though he was still watching me.

She pulled me toward the door.

"Good night, sir," I nodded, just as he squeezed the orange between his fist, shooting an impressive stream of juice into a small glass.

"And Jagger?", he asked, his voice a honeyed song, "Don't do anything I wouldn't do."

When he winked, I hightailed it the fuck out of there.

———

ROXY

My mortification at my dad's behavior prevented me from enjoying Jag's hand on my back as he walked me to his car.

"He still thinks I'm a little girl," I explained lamely as he started the engine "It's been a decade since we've seen each other for more than a couple months a year. He's still not used to the idea of me da—"

Maybe he won't notice that I almost just said "dating".

"—of me doing things on my own, and he thinks that parenting with three times the intensity will make up for all the lost years."

Not so graceful save, I thought as I withered a little in my seat.

"I'd be protective of you, too, Roxy," Jagger said quietly before he pulled onto the road.

The sun had begun to set and it was just past twilight. I had come to worship the darkness of the forest and the embrace of the trees that seemed to guard every inch of road. Jagger's car held his own delectable scent, and the added component of leather was another embrace unto itself. Subdued by the quiet of the engine, the calm of his voice, and the sublime luxury of seat heat, I was lulled into relaxation.

We rode silently at first, and because of the dark, I didn't immediately notice the auxiliary cord. Spotting his shiny black Nano, which I'd been dying to check out, the temptation was too great to resist. Surreptitiously darting my eyes to his face, I made sure his eyes were trained ahead. When I thought the coast was clear, I reached my hand out, to grab it. He got to it first.

"Uh-uh," he tutted as he simultaneously drove, smirked, and scrolled through the device before returning it to the dock. My eyesight was just quick enough to see him initiate a playlist called "concert." When *Ordinary World* by Duran Duran came on, it was my turn to smirk. He'd have seen from stealing my Nano that I loved that song.

"So how'd you score these tickets anyway? I thought they sold out ages ago."

"I was given them as a gift." He shrugged vaguely.

"Someone gave you $1,000 a seat benefit tickets as a gift?" I didn't know what to say. "You gotta introduce me to your friends."

He shrugged again, somewhat uncomfortably.

"My dad's colleague's husband, Greg, writes for Rolling Stone. His editor is a friend of the band and got passes that she couldn't use. She gave them to Greg, who was going to take his wife, but her niece from Sandusky is having some last-minute wedding in Vegas. They know I love Foo Fighters, so they offered the tickets to me. It just happened on Thursday," he spilled out in a rush.

I shook my head and bit my lip to conceal my laughter.

"So, basically your neighbor's cousin's step-uncle is married to Dave Grohl's baby's momma's hairstylist, who just so happens to do your mother's hair, and when she found out you liked the band, she hooked it up?"

As I watched his smile spread to warm his features, I could practically hear the ice breaking.

"Something like that," he said with that velvet chuckle that pulled me a bit deeper each time.

"So...unwelcome parental supervision aside, Roxy...how are you enjoying Rye?"

"The weather's been a little tough," I admitted. "But living with my dad..." I considered my words. "...it's been a good thing."

"So, there's nothing you miss about L.A.?" He frowned a little.

I shrugged, wondering how much I should say about my life there. The kinds of friends I knew and the kind of fun I had there was pretty much the opposite of what anyone knew, or thought, about me in Rye. "I miss my friends, for sure, but it's not like I can go back."

I sensed his hesitation to probe deeper.

"It's complicated," I explained.

"I think I can follow." It was an offer, not a demand.

I realized that maybe I wanted him to know. That, maybe, someone other than Zoë and my dad should.

"I grew up kind of fast," I said glancing over at him. "My mom always wanted to be a singer, but it was hard with a kid, you know? Even without me, it would have been tough going. That's what it's like in L.A."

He looked over briefly, letting me know he was with me, and nodded so I would go on.

"Every small-town talent thinks they're one audition away from their big break. Most people give up after awhile, but my mom never stopped chasing it. And when she found it, she went after it. Getting engaged and booking a spot on a major tour was really great for *her*...."

"But not so great for you?" His voice had a gentle quality to it.

"Last year she moved us to a new school district. I never saw my friends. The tour with Selfish Bliss was the nail in the coffin," I admitted. "She was always on shorter tours on and off when I was a kid, singing backup vocals for a few second-tier bands; she even did cruise ships a few times, you know, when I spent summers with my dad. Her steadiest gig over the years was singing with a 90s nostalgia band whenever we were in L.A...."

"Which explains a lot about your taste in music." He glanced over with a small smile.

"Good taste in music is one of the better things my mom gave me." I shrugged a little.

"And the rest?"

I chose my words carefully. "She would've been the perfect older sister. But I don't think she was cut out to be a mom. She had me when she was eighteen. In a lot of ways, she never grew up. She's...flighty, but kids have practical needs. So, when I was old enough to take care of myself...I did."

He gulped, and I worried that I'd made him uncomfortable, that I'd said too much, too soon.

"How old was old enough to 'take care of yourself'?"

I kept my breathing even.

"Eight."

I noticed his hands tighten on the steering wheel.

"I was six." His adam's apple bobbed before he said it an his voice got a little deep.

When I stared at him in skeptical confusion, his crooked smile was sad.

"It's complicated."

It took me a moment to find my voice.

"I think I can follow."

Even in the dark, I could see his eyes change as he looked ahead.

"I had a baby brother who died when I was that age. My parents kind of...checked out."

The sadness emanating from him in that moment made me want to cry.

"What was his name?" I asked, refusing to toss out a platitude.

"Anthony," he said in a gritty voice. "Anthony," he said again.

THIRTEEN

EVERLONG

Hello, I've waited here
for you, everlong.
Tonight, I throw myself into
and out of the red.
Out of her head, she sang...
-Foo Fighters, *Everlong*

JAGGER

It was hard to believe I'd been nervous about talking to Roxy —it seemed now that I couldn't shut up. It was like that second time we chatted on Instagram, when I lost track of time and the conversation just flowed. I'd worried that our banter, which worked so well online, wouldn't translate to hanging out, face-to-face. If anything, the pull I felt toward her was much stronger in person.

My initial instinct had been correct: there was something different about Roxy that had nothing to do with leather jackets and comically-oversported woolen hats. Only, now I knew why that something different attracted me. God, were we alike. We fell just short of going too 'Dr Phil' on each other on the ride to Seattle, but our conversation stayed pretty deep.

Courtship was new to me, but I was pretty sure that conversation about having to sign your own permission slips because your parents were too out of it to sign them for you wasn't typical first date shit. My compulsion to touch her had only partly to do with my hormones. Four times, I had resisted reaching my hand across the console to commiserate with her silently, maybe by smoothing her hair or by covering her hand with mine.

"Do you like pizza?" I'd just open the door to let her out of my parked car. "My favorite place is right around here."

The show started in an hour, we were a few blocks from The Vermillion Room, and I wanted to make sure she ate.

"Feeding me again, Monroe?"

I loved seeing her blush at something I said, but *fuck*, it was hot when she blushed at herself. It made me wonder whether the thoughts in her pretty, covered head were anything like the forbidden ones in mine.

We made lighter talk as I led the way down streets more crowded than what we were used to. Ft. Bragg was a small beach-front town, which meant that a lot more people than usual were there for the show. I touched her back—to guide her as far as she was concerned, but as a gesture of warning, as far as I was. I didn't like the way men's eyes stopped to appreciate her hip-hugging jeans and the fit of her nubile curves in that tight little hoodie. It was a good thing she was in front of me, chatting away, and unable to see my face as I sent clear signals to those around us.

She. Is. Mine.

We reached the door of the pizza place and she stopped short before walking in, looking inside the window skeptically.

"*This* is your favorite pizza place?"

I looked inside the simple restaurant and saw business as

usual—ten or so partially-gone pies behind glass, customers sitting with their order numbers visible on yellow-top table-booths, a kid at the self-service soda fountain loading up on lemonade.

"Uh, yeah...what's wrong with it?"

"No offense, it's just...I guess I never pegged you as a 'dollar a slice' kind of guy."

Oh, that...

"I'm sure I could find you some more expensive pizza, if it would be more to your liking?" I joked lightly with an ease that surprised even me. Usually, it pissed me off when people judged me for having money, but with Roxy, I found I just wanted to please her.

"I'm sorry—I didn't mean to—" she stammered, and I squeezed her shoulder and laughed.

"Just get inside, Vega."

She ordered the same thing as me—one slice each of regular cheese and one slice of white cheese pizza—and I laughed at her again when she tried to pay. What kind of ass-backwards date did this girl think I was taking her on? We sat across from each other at the table as we waited for our slices to heat. I was taken with the way she played with her straw between taking sips of her soda —it was adorable as hell.

"So, how'd you know I liked Skittles and Coke?"

You drink a Coke Classic at lunch every day and hoard a secret supply of Skittles in your locker, which you only eat when you're stressed out. I was going to give it to you in Civics since you disappeared at lunch, but opportunity knocked.

"Lucky guess..." I shrugged innocently.

I couldn't tell whether she bought it.

"And, how did you know I would like all those songs you added to my iPod?"

I smiled. *So she did like them.*

"Roxy..." I couldn't help leaning in toward her, "It should be abundantly clear by now that we have some kind of..."

Soul-deep connection.

"...*synchronicity* when it comes to music."

The hue of her irises was gorgeous, as was the expression of innocent perplexity on her face. I wanted badly to lean in farther and kiss her, but I could see she hadn't even begun to fathom how deeply I felt for her. It was probably for the best that our pizza came right then. We spent the rest of our meal and our walk to The Vermillion Room gushing about how good the pizza was and one-upping each other on Gunther and Zoë's love struck displays.

The temperature had dropped by the time we approached the venue, and there was a line forming out front. She was just wearing a baby tee under her hoodie, and when I saw her shiver a little I stepped in behind her to rub her shoulders for warmth. We kept on talking, even chatted up some other fans waiting in line. Being with her felt *right*. I diligently alternated rubbing her shoulders and her hands, but twenty minutes later, my girl shivered again. She leaned back toward me—subconsciously, I assumed—in search of more of my warmth.

"Do you want my jacket, Roxy?" I asked softly, dipping my head to speak next to her ear.

By now, her back was on my chest. My hands rubbed her upper arms, and her ear was near my shoulder. She shook her head gently.

"I'm good right here," she whispered.

It was all the invitation I needed to slide my hands down off of her shoulders to fold her inside my arms.

————

ROXY

Waiting outside a club on a cold Seattle night doesn't turn

most people into lust-filled, quivering messes. Then again, most people in front of clubs aren't having their extremities caressed. Most people in front of clubs have had sex recently. Most people in front of clubs aren't busy being dazzled by *Jagger Fucking Monroe.*

I'd lost the capacity to chat up the couple in line in front of us somewhere between the time he started rubbing my fingers and when he pulled me into his chest. I was sure I owed this brand of chivalry only to the blue of Jagger's blood; but I quickly got over why he was doing it and resolved that I would just enjoy. And by enjoy, I meant leaning farther into him, turning my head to the side to better catch his scent, and accepting his embrace. My eyes were closed and I might have been purring, but I was too far gone to care. The self-righteous part of me murmured that he'd better feel lucky I wasn't groping or licking him yet.

I had no sense for how much time had passed as I stood locked inside his arms. The conversations of the crowd and the sounds of traffic registered as a dull roar. I followed the rise and fall of his chest, felt the weight of his chin on my head, felt the sway of his body as he rocked us ever so slightly. It was like floating on the most perfect raft on the bluest ocean on the clearest, most sunny day.

Roxy, love...

Ooh, and I was having the most wonderful fantasies! Now I could hear his voice. Maybe we could—

"Roxy..." he whispered, only this time his voice was real.

It seemed it was time to move. If I didn't know better, I'd think he kissed the top of my head before gently nudging us forward. He kept hold of my hand and the small of my back as he ushered me into the club. The interior was not what I expected.

"They did it in the style of the old supper clubs," Jagger murmured in appreciation, "but the place itself is relatively new."

It was like something out of the movies—a floor-level hardwood dance floor and stage with a bandstand set up behind it, small cocktail tables on the darkly-carpeted floor that encircled the stage, and raised booths that fanned out amphitheater style and were upholstered with fine, vermillion-colored fabric. When I'd heard the show was at a club venue, I'd pictured crowds and beer stench, black-painted walls, speakers that were too loud and filthy bathrooms. But this? This, I would never forget.

An usher seated us in a cozy booth aligned left to the stage and on the closest level to the floor. The set-up had no room for drums, no large amps or enormous speaker sets. I knew the band preferred small venues, but I had no clue this would be such an intimate show. It didn't take long to get everyone seated, and Jagger took my hand as the lights went down.

I was glad he did, because I needed to squeeze *something* when Dave Grohl walked out on stage. I didn't take my eyes off of Dave long enough to see Nate. I barely even heard him talk about LIFEbeat, the charity that had inspired the fundraiser. Though I stayed aware of Jagger's presence, for long moments, it was impossible to fully focus on them both. Instead, I tried not to spontaneously combust from being in the combined presence of the two hottest men on earth.

JAGGER

I tried not to stare at Roxy as she looked in wonder toward the stage. She was grinning widely, her eyes alight with an awestruck joy I had never seen. I loved that being able to see the Foo Fighters made her so happy, loved that I had the good fortune to be in a position to give her this. Plus, the way she paid attention to Dave as he talked about the charity told me she was totally into the cause.

I suspected she was too focused on what the band was saying

to notice my unwavering stare. But since I didn't want to creep her out a second time after the way I'd practically mauled her outside the club, I forced myself to look away, toward the faces of the other fans. It was a beautiful venue that had been tastefully sold out to just the right capacity. Cocktail waitresses floated comfortably among a well-portioned crowd sitting in pairs or threes in rounded booths. Speaking of crowds, I knew this was a small charity show, but shouldn't they have more security? Some of these girls and even a couple of guys looked about ready to pounce on Dave Grohl.

They opened up with a slow, easy version of *Times Like These* that told the crowd just the kind of show this would be. No mega-amps or drums from the band; no screaming or loud applause from the crowd—just gut-wrenching, goose-bumping, soul-filling music.

As it turned out, it wasn't a typical set list—they chose the ones that worked well for a subdued vibe. As the show went on, and they played through *Ain't It The Life*, *February Stars*, and *Hero*, I stopped being so worried about Roxy catching me staring and got pulled into the songs. I'd been to dozens of shows before —always obsessing over having the best seats and getting the best view of the band—but for the first time, it became the most perfect thing in the world to just close my eyes and feel the music.

The times I did have my eyes open, I looked not at the band, but at her. Through *Razor*, *Disenchanted Lullaby*, and a gorgeous version of *Long Road to Ruin*, the most sublime energy flowed inside and around me, and at some point, I realized it wasn't me or the music creating the energy—it was *us*.

What are you doing to me, Roxy?

We didn't speak a word as they played—didn't touch our drinks, but rather sat still with our hands clasped tightly. At times, she closed her eyes or looked at the stage, but sometimes she looked at me like she could peer right into my soul. At those times, I could see her—I mean *really* see her, too—and my girl was fucking beautiful.

I'm falling in love with you.

The realization overwhelmed me, and my eyes fell shut. Few things had ever felt so dangerous, but nothing had felt so right.

I had no concept of how many songs had passed when I heard the opening chords of *Everlong*. I opened my eyes, then, and she was looking at me, and when Dave started singing, I heard the words as if for the first time.

I neither could nor wanted to stop myself from leaning in closer. I whimpered inaudibly as our foreheads touched. My eyes closed as I trailed the end of my nose over the length of hers. My fingers traveled up her arm and neck to caress her slender jaw as I whispered her name against her lips.

Please, love me back, I prayed, breathless, before I caught her lips in a desperate kiss.

FOURTEEN
THIS IS LOVE

I can't believe life's so complex,
when I just want to sit here
and watch you undress.
-PJ Harvey, *This is Love*

ROXY

"Jag," I whispered breathily onto his lips as he pulled back from a searing kiss. I felt drunk as I lifted heavy lids to his smoldering green eyes, a thrill coursing through me as he fixed me with a predatory leer.

"Roxx," he said in a voice that didn't sound like his.

Being with him like this was surreal.

"Roxx..." I heard it again. This time, it was accompanied by a brisk nudge on my shoulder, and it didn't come from Jagger's mouth.

Not yet, Dave! I thought indignantly, *I'll get to you in a minute...*

"Time to shake a leg, kid. I know you got in late last night, but I need to make sure you get up for school."

The best moment of my life fell away as I blinked my eyes awake to find my dad standing above me. I groaned in angry disappointment and threw a stray pillow over my head—I'd pay money to get back into that dream.

"I gotta head out, but coffee's downstairs," came his muffled voice from just beyond the pillow.

I nodded my response, knowing he wouldn't expect more. I was not a morning person.

My limbs were heavy and numb. I felt like I had barely slept, so it took awhile for me to get my bearings. When I registered the sound of the engine of his truck humming into the distance, I was still only marginally awake. I pushed the pillow off of my head, reopened my eyes, and pulled myself up so that I was propped on one arm. Yawning as I ran my fingers through my hair, I spotted something across the room.

His iPod.

And then it all came flying back—Ft. Bragg. The concert. The kiss.

I was up in an instant, all grogginess gone as I practically leapt across the room to my desk. I fingered the special-edition black Nano, smoothing my fingers tentatively over where his name was carved in neat font across the back.

Last night happened.

It wasn't a dream.

I think Jagger and I might be dating.

Then I was grinning, and squealing, and feeling fan-fucking-tastic as I started getting ready for school. Twenty minutes later, I was rocking out hard, my speakers blasting as I belted PJ Harvey into my hairbrush.

"I can't believe life's so complex, when I just want to sit here and watch you undress! I can't believe life's so complex, when I just want to sit here and watch you undress! This is love, this is love that I'm feelin'. This is love this is love, that—"

The music stopped abruptly, but I was on a roll.

"—I'm feelin'. Yeah love, yeah, love."

The lack of music finally registered and I opened my eyes.

"—that I'm feelin'..."

My voice trailed off as I took in Zoë where she stood, dumb-struck, at my bedroom door. Yesterday I would have been embarrassed, but today I burst into a fit of giggles at being caught, at the look on Zoë's face, at the residual ride from the Jagger high. It must have been contagious because she started laughing along with me and soon we were breathless on the floor.

"I already knew your date went well," she said, wiping a tear from her eye, "but I had no idea it went *that* well! Tell me everything!"

And since her catching me like this completely pulled the cat's last limbs from the bag, I did. She hadn't bought it on Friday when I tried to convince the both of us that Jagger had invited me to the concert as a friend. She'd ignored me on Saturday when I'd forbidden her to raid my closet for my hottest pair of skinny jeans. On Sunday, she'd lured me to her house under the guise of telling me about her own first date with Gunther, a story she said she could only recount while doing my hair. Things had gone too far to keep pretending, and I wasn't fooling her anyway. It felt good to let her in.

"He was the perfect gentleman," I gushed. Without telling Jagger's secrets, I told her how we'd talked—really talked—about family and feelings and life. I told her about the modest little pizza place, him keeping me warm in line, the intense gazes and tender touches, and the kiss.

"Oooh, I knew it!" Zoë clapped happily. "See, Roxy? People aren't always what they seem. I knew Jagger was different."

"I guess," I returned pensively, hoping she was right as I rose to my feet and helped her off the floor.

She plopped onto my bed as I put my hairbrush to its intended use.

"So, what did Jagger say to Gunther, exactly?" I asked.

I'll admit it. I was dying to know.

"Nothing. Gunther's very discreet about Jagger," she said, a twinge of disappointment in her voice. "Believe me, I've tried."

"But you said you already knew our date went well. If Gunther didn't tell you, how could you know that?"

"From Jagger."

WTF?

"You talk to Jagger now? Between the hours of one and..." I glanced at my watch. "....eight in the morning?"

Her smile widened as she rolled her eyes.

"Rox-*xy*," she intoned with amused impatience, "I thought you were, like, addicted to Instagram! Didn't you see his update this morning?"

The surprised pause barely lasted a second. I wasted no time tossing my brush onto my desk and diving onto my bed to pull my charging phone off of the bedside table. My heart did a roundoff double back-handspring when I read what he had written. The picture showed a smiling, brown-skinned kid with curly hair, sporting huge green headphones, with his hands up in a posture that made it clear he was dancing. The kid had a dimple and his hans were up and his eyes were closed in enjoyment.

@Moves_like_jagga: Listening to my happy song.

FIFTEEN

BABA O'REILLY

Sally, take my hand.
We'll travel south 'cross land.
Put out the fire
and don't look past my shoulder.
The exodus is here.
The happy ones are near.
Let's get together
before we get much older.
-The Who, *Baba O'Riley*

JAGGER

The only guitar I played was of the air variety, and I was riffing the hell out of my song. I hit play on my computer when I got out of the shower, humming along as I began to get dressed. As the lead guitar kicked in and the tension built and the drums went kind of wild, I jumped onto my bed, wearing no more than socked feet and jeans and laid into the song.

There are many, many things I love about The Who, but nothing more than *Baba O'Reilly*. It's the kind of song that gets you from the very first listen and holds you *right there*. Roger Daltrey started singing the lyrics and I got so into my air guitar that my damp hair fell into my eyes. I was humming along with gusto and getting hopped up on adrenaline, and I barely halted my wild dancing in time for the Pete Townshend part.

Don't cry. Don't raise your eye. It's only teenage wasteland.

Did I mention I play the air drums, too? Well, I do.

"Sally, take my hand. We'll travel south cross land. Put out the fire, and don't look past my shoulder."

That's not Roger Daltrey's voice...

I looked up toward the doorway to find my father rocking his own little air guitar and singing along. I hadn't even heard him come in. He continued singing in earnest. He was kind of dorky, like I imagine most dads are, but at least he had a good voice.

"The exodus is here! The happy ones are near. Let's get together, before we get much older."

I laughed and kicked my feet out from under me, bouncing a little on my behind as I landed on my bed, and took in the vision of my dad letting loose. He was hamming it up so bad we were both cracking up before the song even ended. He strode over to me and clapped my back as he sat down on the bed.

"You're awfully chipper for someone who got home at one in the morning. I take it you had fun at the concert?"

I would normally save such details for Gunther and Deck but I was bursting to tell someone.

"The music, the venue, just *everything*, Dad...it was almost spiritual. It was, like, the best night of my life."

The way my dad looked at me then made me feel that he could read my mind.

"And Roxy? She liked the Food Fighters, too?" he baited.

I suppressed a laugh. My dad wasn't the music aficionado that me and my mom were.

"Uh, dad—I think it's *Foo* Fighters," I corrected kindly. "And, yes, Roxy loved them. She insisted I send her thanks along to Dr. Sturman for passing on the tickets."

He continued cautiously. Dare I say...hopefully? "Roxy. That's a pretty name. She sounds like a nice girl."

"She is a nice girl," I smiled goofily. "Definitely a keeper."

My dad just laughed.

"Well, bring her around any time, son. Your mother and I would love to meet your girlfriend."

The words sent a thrill through my body.

My girlfriend.

I'd never had, or wanted, a girlfriend before, but after last night I knew I wanted something more with Roxy.

"She's not my girlfriend yet, Dad."

But I wanted her to be, and I had no clue how to make that happen. My lack of viable role models was a problem. Annika had initiated things with Declan so he'd be no help, and, for obvious reasons, I couldn't take a leaf out of Gunther's book. In movies, people kissed once and after that they were just *together*. Could it happen like that in real life?

"Then you'll just have to woo her until she begs for the distinction," my dad concluded.

Woo her, I repeated in my mind.

I had to woo Roxy into falling in love.

————

ROXY

"Morning, ladies," Gunther drawled, while grinning pointedly at Zoë as the two of us approached his car.

"Morning, Roxy," Jagger said softly, practically ignoring Zoë as he sported his own smile and I walked to his side.

"Hey, Jag," I replied, my voice suddenly shy, despite my very recent exuberance.

"I brought you this." He extended his hand, which held a Java Hut cup. "And this," he said, reaching for a small paper bag that sat atop his car.

My smile widened and I bit my lip as I took the proffered goods. The warmth from his fingers as they brushed against mine spread throughout my hands.

"I figured you'd be tired from being up so late," he explained, shrugging as if going miles out of the way for coffee on the other side of town wasn't a big deal.

To boot, inside the bag was a toasted bagel with cream cheese. Java Hut didn't toast.

"You got them to toast it?" I asked, eyebrow raised, "How'd you swing that?"

He shrugged again and pulled a second cup of coffee from the roof of his car. "I just asked nicely."

Right.

I shook my head as he sipped his coffee and I took a bite of my bagel.

"Is it good?" he asked a few seconds later.

I just had to laugh.

"You know, your obsession with me eating is borderline manic," I quipped. "I eat every day. Like, a lot."

He shot me a crooked smirk, and something lit in his eyes. It reminded me of the night before, and I blushed.

"Prove it," he challenged.

"Prove that I eat?"

"Sit with me at lunch."

And so another morning was spent paying no attention to my classes as I daydreamed about Jagger. I wondered what he thought our status was, and how he knew I liked medium cream and heavy sugar. At least this week there were a few things I was sure of. At least I knew how he kissed. My mind drifted back to the night before...

The music had transformed him. That had been easy enough to see. He'd been dropping his defenses all night, but from the opening notes of the set, he'd visibly relaxed. His lips had melted into a serene smile. His thumb had stroked gently across the back of my hand. And his eyes—normally so sharp and attentive—had lulled closed in intermittent surrender.

You are beautiful.

I'd thought it over and over, marveling first at his pretty face until I'd admitted there was so much more. As the music had swirled around us, I'd considered all I'd learned of him that night: what had been taken from him, where he'd learned to fend for himself, how he'd survived. I knew now that beneath that hard candy shell was a kid who had overcome bad circumstances to become a kind, sharp, witty, and decent human being. My mantra changed.

You are extraordinary.

The music had kept playing, spiraling me deeper into my trance; and when our eyes had locked and we'd gazed unabashedly, all was right. What I'd seen in his eyes—respect, adoration, understanding—hadn't scared me. The promise of intimacy with him had only drawn me in. This man had touched me and looked at me and reached me like no one ever had, like I'd never even wanted anyone else to do.

Come with me.

And when he'd leaned in, so slowly, to share my breath, to caress my face and neck, he'd whispered something against my lips, like a secret. I had never been kissed like he kissed me then, as if he consumed me with every tug of his lips and sweep of his tongue. He'd been thorough and slow, but chillingly intense. I'd shuddered, my head weaving a bit after we'd pulled apart, our foreheads meeting again as we'd caught our breath. And, when he'd kissed me again, I was whole. I'd prayed, then, for continuation, for a future that stretched beyond that night, that kiss, that song.

Never stop, Jag. Please, never stop.

————

JAGGER

French with Madame Smith was less than engaging on the best of days, but today, *je m'en fous*. I wasn't a model student, but at least I paid attention in class. That is, until I got involved with Roxy Vega.

I couldn't stop—didn't want to stop—reliving the most fantastic night of my life...the deepest connection, the most breathtaking kiss, and the most delicious promise for more. We'd gotten back to her place so late, but neither of us was tired. I would have driven another hundred miles for more time hearing her soft voice, more stories about her life, and the feeling of holding her hand. As we pulled up to Roxy's house at 12:45 AM, the lights were on downstairs. She rolled her eyes.

"He waited up." The front curtains rustled as she said the words.

I'd been afraid of this. Afraid that the watchful eye of her father would block me from what I wanted to do. I'd wanted to walk her to her door and give her a long, proper kiss and tell her I hoped she'd let me take her out again soon. Since that had been out of the question, I'd had to resort to Plan B: a subtler signal of my intentions.

"Can I borrow your iPod?"

Her eyebrows had risen. I must've really caught her off guard. Shutting down the part of myself that wanted to figure out whether there was some other obvious or appropriate thing I was supposed to say in this moment, I'd forged ahead with my plan.

"Roxy," I chuckled in a way I hope concealed my nerves, "I

was going to let you borrow mine. You keep trying to get at it, so I figured..."

I'd shrugged as she pieced it together, looking surprised, then smug.

"'Bout time you lent me yours. I was hours away from kidnapping it. There was gonna be a ransom note and everything."

I'd laughed then, for real.

"Whatever, Vega. Just trade me now and we'll give them back next time."

"Next time?"

"You know..." I'd replied hopefully, not so much a statement as a question. "Next time we go out?"

She'd nodded and given me one of those bit-lip smiles, and I'd resisted the urge to kiss her while she'd fished for her silver Nano. I'd worn a shit-eating grin as I'd helped her from the car, walked her to her front door, and given her a regrettably brief hug.

"Good night, Roxy." I'd kissed her forehead.

"Good night, Jagger," she'd said sweetly.

I'd grinned all the way home.

Between how we'd left things the night before and my dad's advice that morning, my mission was clear: ask Roxy out. But I'd been too nervous at lunch (I wasn't crazy about doing it in front of an audience), and once we got to Civics, I knew it would be lame to do it again via passed note, so I'd played it cool and chatted her up about other stuff. I'd tested her, too, with little touches and gestures, searching for confirmation that she still wanted my attention. By the end of Civics, I'd been fairly certain she'd say yes to my proposition, so I'd asked whether I could walk her to her next class.

"So, do you have plans on Wednesday? Like, right after school?"

She'd set her mouth like someone pretending to think.

"Other than rearranging all the songs on your iPod? No."

My answering glare had only been half-joking.

"Don't blow a gasket, Monroe—I'm just kidding."

"Not funny, Roxanne." But I was half-smiling now.

She'd nudged me playfully as we walked.

"So do you want to hang out with me on Wednesday, or what?" I'd asked feigning mild impatience before softening my voice. "I thought we could chill for a few hours, maybe listen to some music..."

More than a few passing students had taken notice of us by then, though I'd doubted they could hear our conversation.

"It depends," she'd said, stopping in front of her classroom.

"Are you gonna come up with a condition *every* time I ask you on a date?" I'd asked honestly.

Her eyes had widened for a second before her face melted into a smile.

"Tell me your happy song from this morning," she'd demanded.

That's her condition? I'd shaken my head and smiled.

"Gimme my iPod," I'd said.

"No way!" she'd retorted. "I have it 'til Wednesday."

"So you *are* going out with me?" I'd smiled.

"Only if you tell me your happy song," she'd insisted.

"Then, gimme my iPod!" I'd laughed.

"Who's on first," she'd stated indignantly.

Then I'd really laughed. This girl was *funny*.

"Roxy," I'd said slowly, as if I were talking to a child. "If you give me my iPod for just a second, I will put the song on for you."

Recognition had dawned on her face as she'd handed it over, looking sheepish. She'd put the ear buds in as I'd located the song. The bell had been about to ring.

"See you Wednesday, Roxy."

Yeah, I know. I'd see her tomorrow. Hopefully chat with her tonight, even. But I'd wanted her to start thinking about

Wednesday already—wanted it to consume her every thought like it would consume mine. Her answering blush had sent confidence surging through me.

This is happening. This is really happening, I'd thought giddily while keeping my cool for her benefit, of course.

I'd winked as I pressed play.

SIXTEEN

BAD REPUTATION

I know I got a bad reputation,
and it isn't just talk, talk, talk.
If I could only give you everything
you know I haven't got...
-Freedy Johnston, *Bad Reputation*

ZOË

Roxy clutched the door grip as I veered into the Chevron gas station parking lot at a speed that some might consider fast. We were running a little early for school, so I figured I'd fill my tank. I screeched to a stop and hopped out to pump gas.

No sooner had I tapped my phone to the console to Apple Pay for my gas than did Roxy emerge with a yawn. She really wasn't a morning person and I didn't need a crystal ball to know she was headed into the mini-mart for coffee.

"Tranquilizer shot?" she offered sardonically.

It had become our little joke. Roxy was too polite not to offer to get me something if she was grabbing something for herself, but she'd officially banned me from caffeine. I flipped her the bird, which earned me a laugh before she turned and walked into the store. I, too, was smiling by the time I chose a high octane grade and stuck the nozzle in the opening of the tank.

Leaning against my car, I let the gas flow, shifting my eyes to watch my friend as she moved through the store. *She's so happy with him,* I thought. Her face said it all. Since she'd started flirting with Jag, it had brightened her smile by lumens.

I didn't like to be the one to say "I told you so," but I'd always seen there there was something between them. I hadn't foreseen that it would be this strong. Gunther said he could feel that they were in love. I was certain they'd end up together, but Roxy was still unsure of so many things. Not only with Jagger, that girl had a serious confidence problem. She lived life on the outside, listening to her music and reading her books. She stood on the sidelines at roller derby, cheering us on but never in the game; always a bridesmaid but never a bride. I'd been trying for ages to pull her out of her shell. I liked to think she'd improved in the months she'd been here. But, somehow, Jagger was making a difference.

A big old noisy truck pulled in on the other side of the filling island, blocking my view of Roxy and the mart. As they exited the cab, I recognized the voices of two boys from our school. I couldn't see their faces from over the station, which meant they couldn't see mine.

"What do you expect, man? No one had a chance at popping that cherry but Monroe. I'm just glad he's doing it now so the rest of us can have a turn."

They're talking about Roxy!

"I don't know, dude. He looks pretty into her. You might be waiting awhile to hit that."

I stood, mortified, as I heard the little beeps of the machine as one of them pressed buttons and pre-paid to get his gas.

"Of course he looks into her—it's all part of the act. He can turn it on and off like a faucet. I'd almost admire the guy if he wasn't such a douche."

My eyes filled up with angry tears, and I prayed that Roxy was still in the store.

"He's smooth alright, but I still think you're wrong. Sure, he wants to fuck her—shit, *everyone* wants to fuck her—but dating girls isn't his M.O."

When the first guy laughed, I had half a mind to walk around the pump and tell them from what. The sound of the metallic click that signaled that my own tank was full interrupted my thoughts. I entertained a brief fantasy of yanking the nozzle free and dousing the assholes on the other side of the pump with gasoline. No need to light them on fire. I'd settle for a chemical burn. By the time I walked around the pump, both of them had moved to walk into the mini mart. I started after them, still bent on giving both a piece of my mind.

"Don't."

But Roxy's voice stopped me. I hadn't seen her come back out. Apparently, neither had they. I knew then we wouldn't make it to first period—that we might not even make it to school. Driving in silence, I took us to an out-of-the-way park. It was too early for moms to be out with their kids. I let her lead the way and wasn't surprised when she walked us toward the swings. We swayed gently, and I let her begin.

"I need to you to tell me everything again, Zoë. And, not your interpretation—I need the facts."

I'd once told her about him, months ago when she'd first arrived.

"During freshman year, he slept with the Homecoming Queen. They were caught in someone's bedroom, over spring break, at a party. They weren't together—it was just a hookup. But it didn't matter. He was freshman that bedded the most popular girl in school. By graduation, he was running with this kid, James. James wasn't jock-popular—he was bad boy popular. And he taught Jagger everything he knew."

"It started the summer before our sophomore year, the summer before James' senior year. And it wasn't just Jagger, Roxy —Declan and Gunther got caught up in it, too. I never went to any of their parties or saw anything firsthand. But, whatever did or didn't happen didn't look good. I saw one girl Jag supposedly slept with curse him out in the middle of the hallway and another turn a cafeteria tray over his head. It made all the rumors credible. Declan and Gunther got it to a lesser degree. But the leader always seemed to be Jagger."

"And James?" Roxy's expression gave nothing away.

"James graduated last year. Everyone figured Jagger would become king bad boy, even though he's only a junior. But Declan started dating Annika over the summer, and Gunther and Jagger toned it down. You've only been here for less than a year. People still talk, but it's nothing like it was."

Roxy didn't speak for a long time, and we both swayed in small circles on the swings. I had to bite the inside of my cheek to keep from saying more. I knew she had doubts and I itched for her to ask the next logical question. I waited, impatiently, for her to open the door.

"Why all of a sudden?"

Huh. I didn't expect that.

"Gunther's been following you like a puppy for ages," she continued. "But out of the blue, Jagger suddenly likes me. It just doesn't make sense."

"Don't edit history, Roxx," I scolded. "I told you for months that Jagger had a thing for you, just like you said the same about Gunther. The only recent thing is that both of them stopped being freaks about it and manned up to ask us out."

She looked skeptical.

"But, doesn't it bother you to know that Gunther used to be..."

She was too polite to say it.

"A manwhore?" I supplied. "We've talked about it, and he's not proud. But he can't change his past, and neither can Jagger. People aren't perfect, Roxy. But they can change."

She turned to look at me fully.

"But what if Jagger hasn't changed? What if he's exactly the same, and I'm just too naive to see it?"

I rolled my eyes.

"Jagger is not the same, Roxy. He walks you to class and sends you candy-grams at pep rallies. He hands you coffee and a bagel in front of the whole school. He flirts with you on Instagram and makes you playlists and takes you to concerts most people can't even get tickets to."

"Maybe it's part of the act," she said, her voice empty and mechanical as she quoted gas station asshole number one.

"Maybe you're different, since dating women isn't part of his standard M.O." I shot back, quoting asshole number two.

She sighed.

"Look, Roxy. I know you're scared. But you can't fight the fear with sabotage. You can't write him off or judge him for who he used to be. Decide whether you want him based on who he is today. And, let me venture a guess: you've never caught him in a lie. And he's never done anything suspicious."

She gave a reluctant nod.

"Then, stop condemning him, Roxy. Let him be innocent until proven guilty."

SEVENTEEN
SHAKE IT OFF

'Cause the players gonna
play, play, play, play, play.
The haters gonna hate,
hate, hate, hate, hate.
I'm just gonna shake,
shake, shake, shake, shake.
I shake it off, I shake it off.
-Taylor Swift, *Shake it Off*

ROXY

I was trying desperately not to laugh out loud at the things Jagger whispered in my ear, but his running commentary on Gunther and Zoë was too funny. They sat across from us at the lunch table ,heavily immersed in the sickly-sweet oblivion reserved for the deeply in love. Over the past week, we'd witnessed our share of minor PDAs, but they were starting to forget they were in public. At present, Jagger and I were each eating our own slices of pizza while Gunther and Zoë shared the same one.

"Cheese pizza, $3.00," Jagger said quietly between bites in a commercial announcer voice.

We watched as Gunther took his own small bite before angling the slice to feed Zoë. I hid my smile behind my napkin, sharing a brief, knowing look with Jagger as I pretended to wipe my mouth.

"Side of Tater Tots, $2.00," he continued dramatically when Gunther squeezed a thick bead of ketchup from a little Heinz packet onto a crispy tot. Gunther smiled sensually as he pushed it through Zoë's waiting lips and nipped a nonexistent ketchup remnant from his finger.

By then I was giggling under my breath and looking back at Jagger's sage-colored eyes which now sparkled beautifully with humor. He had an extraordinary ability to keep his face mostly neutral, which made his hint of a smile even sexier.

"Pudding cup, $1.50," he said, his voice still smooth.

I looked behind my shoulder at the mention of the pudding cup, knowing what was about to happen but needing to see it myself. I felt my chair turn slightly and I realized that Jagger had angled me away from their view, and in doing so pulled me towards him. My tiny gasps as I caught my breath were suddenly filled with more of his scent.

"Having sex with your clothes on in the middle of a crowded lunch room..."

My head fell onto his shoulder as I snorted quietly. He now shook in muted laughter.

"Priceless," he gasped.

I grasped his forearm, still trying to keep it together. The hard muscle under his soft skin felt better than nice. After collecting myself, I glanced back at Gunther and Zoë. They remained oblivious.

"Unbelievable," I muttered, wiping an escaped tear and

smiling back up at Jagger. His façade had broken, and now he was grinning—that crooked, beautiful grin.

"I don't know what *you two* think is so funny," came Annika's voice from the other side of the table. "You're almost as bad as they are."

Her lips were curled in her signature smirk. Only Declan was laughing now.

She was right, of course. Jagger and I had grown close. He almost made me forget my fears. It now felt natural to walk together to class, to text every day and Instagram every night. A few people thought we were collateral to the Gunther and Zoë romance, but to astute observers like Annika, that was clearly not the case. Given that we'd never so much as held hands in public, I'd thought we were being discreet. But, between those assholes at the gas station and Annika's comment now, I fully grasped that people were taking notice.

If only it were his past that had sounded alarms. Zoë brushed my other worry aside whenever I mentioned it: Jagger and I had history of our own. It was easy to forget that things between us hadn't always felt so right, but the facts could not be denied: for six months, there'd been nothing. Not a word in Civics class. Barely a civil response to my attempts at being nice.

Then, suddenly, one day he'd decided he wanted to me my friend. And instead of telling him where he could stick his friendship, I'd let him. The questions remained: What had prompted his change of heart? The easiest assumption to make was that the gossip was true, that people had seen him do this before. It was inconsistent with the Jagger of the past ten days, but it rang possible for the Jagger of the past six months.

But I couldn't afford to make hasty assumptions. There was more than just me at stake. The Gunther/Zoë union had married our cliques, and any serious rift between Jagger and me would spell trouble. It made me wish I knew where we stood. I would rather he tell me straight if he was just after a hookup or if he was flirting casually out of sheer boredom. It had occurred to me I may have been the next natural choice for a companion since he'd lost his best friend to mine.

And what about the other explanation, the one I barely even let myself consider: what if I wasn't just a conquest? What if he wanted more? I'd never had one before, but this was how it was supposed to work. Guys you were attracted to and liked a lot became *boyfriends*. I hated myself for even wishing for something like that when I had so many other doubts.

The end of lunch and the walk to Civics were mostly uneventful. I tried to be normal, but these thoughts plagued my mind. Halfway through class, Jagger slipped me a note.

Are you OK? You're totally spacing.

I gave him a little nod and tried to smile. Frowning, he took back his paper and scribbled another note.

Would you tell me if you weren't?

When I looked back at him, he was blatantly ignoring the lecture, his face worried and maybe a little sad. I grabbed the paper, not wanting to look in his eyes for fear he would see too much.

Probably.

It wasn't a lie. This issue aside, I *would* tell him what was bothering me. *Yeah, I'm pretty screwed,* I thought again as I pretended to re-engage in the lecture. I pretended not to notice him watching me surreptitiously, pretended I couldn't practically hear the wheels turning in his head. Minutes later, he wrote another message and slid it to me slowly.

You can talk to me about anything, Roxy.

But I couldn't talk to him about this. I could see the note I might pass back to him now: *Do you like me for real or are you stringing me along? No bullshit. Circle one: Yes or No.* But instead of writing *that* note, I just mouthed my thanks, no clearer on what to do.

————

JAGGER

It was the middle of seventh period and the end of the day couldn't come soon enough. In ninety minutes, we'd be leaving for our date. I'd spent every free minute that week hanging out, texting, and chatting with Roxy, but I couldn't wait to get her alone. From the time I woke up to the time I fell asleep, she was on my mind. I even spent yesterday afternoon in NICU telling Nick more about her during our cuddle. I'd been dropping hints all week that I wanted to make it official, but I didn't know where we stood.

Foo Fighters concert notwithstanding, I got the sense she wasn't the PDA type, so I'd kept things at school subtle and clean. But I had started touching her more and coming close into her space, and she never flinched or shied away. No. Roxy blushed when I whispered in her ear; she let me walk her to class. I even carried her books once or twice. She didn't stop me on Tuesday when I snaked fries from her lunch tray, and when she finished her Coke, she started drinking mine.

As an added bonus, the boys at school seemed to be getting the picture. Her usual cadre of hopeful suitors had backed off. But I got the sense that something was going on with her.

I'm bored.

I glanced down at my phone, which had vibrated with a new text from Roxy. When I pictured her bored face, I smiled.

At least Mr. Fenicle's class is just boring. Mrs. Berardi's voice grates on my nerves, I replied.

I tried to look engaged as I waited for her next text. Surreptitiously texting in class was an art.

"Just" boring? If I had a suicide pill in my pocket, I'd use it. I can't take this anymore!

I stifled a laugh when she followed up with the yellow emoji that had a letter x over each eye.

Please Miss Vega, not that! Perhaps I can come to your aid...

I had an idea. I fired off the text before slipping my phone in my pocket and raising my hand.

"Yes, Mr. Monroe?" Mrs. Berardi ground out in her annoyingly-high voice. I plastered on a charming smile.

She was thirty-five and married, albeit to a younger man, and known to be quite the puma. Declan, Gunther and I had compared notes and she'd hit on all three of us. This would be embarrassingly easy.

"May I be excused early, Mrs. Berardi? I have a dentist appointment in Littleton at three."

Her eyes traveled my body.

"Yes, go ahead Jagger. And bring a note next time."

"Thank you." I smiled sweetly as I gathered my things, dodging hostile, knowing glances from the other students as I walked out.

EIGHTEEN
CHASING CARS

If I lay here, if I just lay here,
Would you lie with me
and just forget the world?
-Snow Patrol, *Chasing Cars*

ROXY

It was after-school-date day with Jagger, and the wall clock couldn't tick fast enough. Even under the best of circumstances, it would have felt like a long wait. But these *weren't* the best of circumstances. I hated this class and there were still twenty minutes left. I had texted Jagger to help pass the time, but he'd dropped off in order to "come to my aid." I couldn't imagine what he could do, short of pulling a fire alarm, to get me out of this hell. I was busy doodling elaborate graffiti—things like "RV+JM" and "Kill Me Now." Then I'd scribble all over it, lest anyone else ever find it, only to start again on the next blank corner of page.

The phone in the classroom rang and the students let out a collective sigh. How long could we listen to Mr. Fenicle drone on about the Lend-Lease Act? The man never asked questions or engaged the class to participate. There were times he even read aloud from the book!

"Miss Vega?" he said, fixing his eyes on me even before hanging up the phone, "Please see Mrs. Cole in the office, and take your things. You have an early dismissal."

No fucking way, I thought, as I packed up my bags and headed into the hall.

Through the glass doors of the office, I saw Jagger leaning over and chatting up Mrs. Cole. They were laughing as if they were old friends. She didn't notice me opening the door, but Jagger noticed me right away.

"Roxy, you're so silly sometimes. How could you forget again?" he asked in a playfully-patronizing voice, punctuating his question with a wink. "I was just telling Mrs. Cole how you make us late every time."

I was a little slow to the uptake, but I could be a smooth liar when I needed to be.

"You know how I hate to leave early from History. Mr. Fenicle's lecture was so interesting, I forgot to look at the clock." I looked at Mrs. Cole sorrowfully. "Sorry you had to call me out of class."

"No problem, dear. Jagger explained the whole situation. You'd better get started if you want to make your appointments. You wouldn't want cavities to ruin your smile," she lectured gently, beaming over at Jagger.

"Thank you again, Mrs. Cole. You're a real life saver," he smiled, knocking the desk once before ushering me out.

As soon as we were in the parking lot, he grabbed my book bag from my arm and slung it over his opposite shoulder before sliding his hand into mine. He bit back a grin, saying nothing until we got into his car.

"To Littleton, Ms. Vega?" he asked like a chauffeur.

"Is that where our dentist appointments are, *Ferris*?" I

smirked.

"Yes. We schedule our monthly check-ups back to back so we can carpool."

"How lovely of us to reduce our carbon footprint... and, *monthly* appointments? We must have the cleanest teeth in Rye."

"Good dental hygiene is very important, Roxy."

I just shook my head as we sped out of the lot, duly impressed by how effortlessly he'd pulled it off and discomfited that he'd just conned three teachers. The next hour was spent in comfortable conversation, but I began to quiet as we got into town. Jagger navigated streets in an offbeat neighborhood I had never seen. It was near a boat marina, but away from the most popular shopping streets. The shops here were less upscale than the ones I went to with Zoë. As he pulled over to park, I figured out where we were going.

"Plastic Fantastic?" I smirked at the name.

"Have you ever been here?" he asked, sounding hopeful that I hadn't.

I shook my head. "I didn't even know this was here."

"I think you're gonna love it." He smiled excitedly. "I practically live here on weekends."

Before I had my seatbelt off, he was at my door, taking my hand as he helped me from the car. He didn't let it go as we walked through the front door, speaking rather than waving his hello to the store clerk that greeted him by name. Plastic Fantastic turned out to be an enormous record store that sported thousands (perhaps tens of thousands) of LPs. I stood near the door in wonder. I hadn't been to an honest-to-goodness record store since I was little. Still, I felt completely at home.

"Do you own any vinyl?" Jagger asked, noticing my reaction.

"I used to. Or at least my mom did."

He showed me around the store, teaching me about how to

buy vinyl, telling me how the sign of a great music store was organization. I lost sense of time as we browsed together, picking out a mix of titles—some that Jag said he was dying for me to hear, and others I remembered listening to with my mom. By the time we reached the counter, arms laden with records, it occurred to me that for someone who didn't have a record player, I was planning to buy quite a lot. Jagger gave me a quizzical look as I set my choices on the counter.

"Do you mind if we take number three?" he asked the clerk.

"It's all yours." The guy handed Jagger a key.

Jagger scooped up my records as well as his own and nodded his head towards some stairs in the back. I followed him up and was met by four numbered rooms.

Listening booths, I realized with delight.

Following Jagger through the last door on the left, I saw these were no regular booths. They were small rooms, each with a record player and two chairs, and their walls were made of glass. The placement on the second floor right over the water made it so we could not only listen to records but also look out at the bay.

"What do you think?" he asked, studying my face as I took in the afternoon view.

I turned to him and smiled.

"I can see why you live here on weekends."

JAGGER

It was already the perfect date. I'd impressed her at every turn. I'd broken her out of her Mr. Fenicle-induced jail. I'd sounded casual and smooth when we'd talked on the drive. I'd been in awe of the mellow look on her face as we'd listened to music at Plastic Fantastic. I'd taken her to a café for a snack. Now, it was almost sunset and I'd driven her to another place I came to all the time.

It was an oceanside bluff I'd stumbled across months before while exploring one of the many regional parks. My favorite spot had a few picnic tables and stayed pretty empty this time of year. I'd brought a big blanket for us to cuddle under and that was exactly what we were doing. I leaned against the narrow end of the picnic table with Roxy's back to my front. The dark gray wool blanket was pulled across the back of my body and I circled her in my arms.

It was both comforting and terrifying—how we molded together so easily in moments like this. I wished I could keep thoughts of the other moments at bay. There was something she wasn't telling me. I fell into a pensive state as I felt more than listened to her breathe against my chest. As we stared out at the ocean in descending twilight, the cool wind chilling our faces, I couldn't stop the words.

"You're such a mystery, Roxy."

It was a source of both pain and intrigue. I loved everything that made her different, but feared that she may never let me in. I was so used to people being transparent to me—used to the girls at school being eager to do all the talking.

"Are you kidding?" She chuckled sadly. "You pepper me with questions and I answer them all. You, on the other hand, give away nothing."

I tried not to let her words sting. I'd showed her everything that mattered about me. The rest was superficial. If I could just show her she was the only one...

"Hey, I'm sorry." She broke me out of my thoughts.

"You don't have to apologize for anything."

Hadn't I just wished for her to not censor herself with me?

"No, I do have to." She closed her eyes for a moment, as if pained. "I know you've told me some really important things about you. But there's other stuff—lots of it—that I just don't understand."

"Like what?"

I tried to make it sound like I wasn't begging, but I was.

"You're just...not who I thought you'd be."

Oh. That.

"Based on what people say about me?"

I'd been so paranoid about other grist for the Trinity High rumor mill, I'd never considered what Roxy herself thought of my reputation.

"That, " she admitted. "And...no offense, but we sat next to each other for months. You never noticed me at all."

"I *always* noticed you, Roxy," I said with conviction. "But I was too stupid and too shy to approach you. And it wasn't just you I ignored—by the time you moved to Rye, I'd pretty much written off everyone but Deck and Gunther."

She nodded, though I didn't think she quite believed me.

"Why did you change your mind?"

I didn't. Declan changed my mind for me, I absolutely could not say. It wasn't just that I couldn't force the words out—somehow, I just knew the real story would change things. So I told a lie of omission.

"It took strength to stay away from you, Roxy. One day, I just...caved."

I didn't know whether to be disgusted or relieved by how convincing I sounded. Doubtful that I could live with myself if I lied any more, I cut her off before she could respond.

"Here's the thing, Roxy. I let people think what they want to think because I don't care about them or what they say. But I do care about you, Roxy. And if I've let anyone know me, it's been you."

She nodded again, looking only a little more convinced.

"I've never brought any girl to watch the sun set, or taken any girl to Plastic Fantastic. Before Sunday, I never went on a one-on-one date or met a girl's dad. I never wanted to call anybody my girlfriend."

Her breathing caught.

"You know me, Roxy," I insisted once again. "Tell me what you do know about me, Roxy. You know a lot."

Please, I thought as my heartbeat quickened. I needed this to work.

"Well, you have phenomenal taste in music..." She bit her lip. "For some strange reason, you're obsessed with feeding me."

The corner of her mouth turned up in a smile.

"What else?" I whispered. I needed to know that she understood.

"You have a weird sense of humor. You pay attention to, like, everything. And you seem to like keeping me warm."

She really doesn't get it.

"Is that really all you know about me? I thought I gave so much more away."

I tightened my arms around her again, glad she was looking out at the ocean.

"I was sure you noticed how much I laugh when I'm with you...and how much I love making you blush."

She did just that. My heartbeat quickened as I debated whether to say it. She had such an impairing effect on my judgment...

"And on Sunday, it should've been pretty obvious that I could die happy from kissing you."

Though she tensed slightly at first, her body leaned closer into mine.

"How can I believe you didn't know those things?" I asked desperately as I dropped a kiss below her ear.

Her eyes fell shut and her breathing changed, and I knew that now was my time. She didn't resist as I turned her in my arms, and she opened her brown eyes to meet mine. She said nothing, only tipped up her chin. It was the only invitation I needed.

In the three days since I'd known her luscious mouth, I'd thirsted for her kiss. My greed to devour her found me kissing her deeply. My need to have her found me pulling her body flush against mine. This time there were no first kiss jitters, no cocktail table or awkward sitting position to keep us apart. This time, we were all alone. No need to be discreet. No reason not to let my hand slide over the curve of her bottom. Catching my breath as I nipped her ear, her jaw, her neck, I realized that our "kiss" had escalated by fathoms.

It wasn't until my mind followed the throbbing source of my pleasure that I realized I was painfully, conspicuously, hard. Since I was leaning on the table, I pushed her hips away a little, but she protested loudly—not saying a word but grinding her pelvis into mine. And then her hands were in my hair and her eyes were filled with lust and she captured my lips one more time.

Fuuuuuuck!

I learned much about my Roxy as the sun set that day. I memorized the taste of her skin. I became intimately familiar with the curve of her breast and the sound of her whimpering moan. I knew the whisper of my name on her lips. And I then learned something else: when it came to the lies they told about Roxy, her rap was as bogus as mine.

My almost-girlfriend was anything but frigid or prudish. She was sensual and alive. She kissed like she had invented the art, and her touch made me purr. At times I pulled back, in case she needed space, but she proved she didn't want it. Roxy seemed to want me as much as I wanted her. So much for taking it slow.

NINETEEN

IS IT OKAY IF I CALL YOU MINE?

Is it okay if I call you mine, just for a time?
And I will be just fine if I know that you
know that I'm wanting, needing your love.
-Paul McCrane, *Is it Okay if I Call You Mine*
(From the Original Soundtrack of the
movie *Fame*)

JAGGER

It had only been four hours since I dropped her off at home, but already I missed her fiercely. By the time I gathered the courage to pick up the phone and call, it was past eleven. Dogged by disappointment, I settled for second best: a look at whether she'd updated her Instagram page. Defaulting to my favorite guilty pleasure when I saw she had not, I went straight to the pictures she'd been tagged in, from her profile.

My favorite, the one of her with a guitar in a cracked desert surrounded by canyons, always made me smile. A light sprinkling of freckles speckled her nose, a contented little smile puckered her lips, the rise of stray wisps of her long hair told of a dry wind, and she looked straight at the camera. The guitar was shiny and black, and it deepened her eyes—a perfect contrast against to reds and oranges of the desert. I had studied the picture for hours, and I would study it again. It always took me to sweet dreams.

After I'd had my fill and was about to plug in my phone, a text came in from Roxy.

Too keyed up to sleep.

I tapped out my reply immediately.

Me, too. There's someone I can't get off my mind.

But she was so adorable, and I'd missed her so much that I had to pick up the phone and call.

"Shall I hum you a lullaby?" I asked.

She laughed. I hadn't even waited for her to say a greeting.

"Tell the truth, Jagger. Are you some kind of Stepford droid?"

I didn't know what the hell she was talking about, but in that moment I loved her voice. It was soft, perhaps so as not to wake up the chief. Either that or her mood changed when she was in bed. I got a little hard imagining what she must be wearing. I suppressed the urge to ask.

"What's wrong with lullabies?" I asked instead.

"If you sang me a lullaby it would fuel my suspicion that you're freakishly perfect."

"I play the piano, too." I offered.

"See? Now you're just trying to impress me."

"You caught me. Is it working?"

I held my breath.

"Yes," she whispered.

Euphoria.

"Will you come over one day so I can play for you?"

Her voice was low and sultry when she said, "Only if you show me your room."

My hand that wasn't holding the phone slid down to restrain

my cock. *It's okay, boy,* I appeased it gently. *Don't freak out—she's only teasing.*

"Are you trying to kill me, Ms. Vega?"

"You caught me. Is it working?"

My chuckle held a hint of desperation. "At this rate, I'll be dead by Friday."

Our talk in Littleton had really moved the ball, and I was awed by this new side of Roxy. It felt more and more like she was being herself. I loved seeing evidence that she was getting more comfortable with me, loved the little ways she showed me her trust. I hadn't realized until today how much she'd held back.

"I guess I'd better hear you play tomorrow, then."

"Sorry, love." I said sadly, "I'm busy." The patients at the hospital needed me.

"Maybe next week then." She sounded a little deflated.

Screw that.

"How about Friday? You could come over then."

"Aren't Fridays when you hang out with Gunther and Declan?"

"Everyone can come over—we'll make it a triple date. They won't mind."

Sound casual.

"You could even meet my parents."

Act like it's not a big deal. Wait, no! Act like it is *a big deal. Because it is.*

"They really want to meet you, Roxx. They've been bugging me to have you over for dinner."

Shit. That sounded like my parents wanted her there more than me.

"But I really want to have you for dinner, too."

Seriously, Jagger. Shut the hell up.

"You told your parents about me?" Thank God she sounded more surprised than pissed off or weirded out.

"Of course I did." By then my voice had calmed.

"Alright, I'll come over. How about after school? You promised you'd play the piano."

And it hit me then. In just two days time, Roxy would be serving more than a brief visit—I'd have her at my house for hours. She would eat in my dining room and sit next to me on my piano bench. She would enter the bat cave and touch all my things. She may even lie on my bed. Visions of her sprawled out and ready for me assaulted my mind as I thought of continuing where we'd left off earlier that day.

Sweet Jesus...

"And I will," I promised, struggling to keep the raging erection out of my voice. "But now that we have that settled, you should really be going to bed. I just called to say a quick good night."

"Night, Jag." She yawned, her fatigue striking right on time. "Sweet dreams."

"I'll see you in the morning, my Roxy."

TWENTY

BEST DAY OF MY LIFE

I'm never gonna look back.
Whoa, never gonna give it up.
No, please don't wake me now.
-American Authors, *Best Day of My Life*

ROXY

"Ready?" Jagger called to me warmly as he approached where Zoë and I were sitting atop a picnic bench. He held out his hand in an offer to help me down. Ignoring the interested stares of our classmates, I kept my eyes on him. He didn't break his gaze until our hands were joined and his kiss brushed the top of my fingers.

"Your chariot awaits." He smiled as I stepped down from the bench and slung his arm over my shoulder. I didn't miss Zoë's triumphant smile as I nuzzled into his neck. Once Gunther slung her messenger bag over his own shoulder and got Zoë on piggyback, we four beat a lazy retreat across the quad and toward the cars.

"How were the paparazzi today?" Jagger asked, squeezing my shoulder protectively.

In the two days since we'd gone public with our relationship, things had been unreal. The searing kiss he gave me in the parking lot the morning after Littleton had taken Trinity High by storm. People passed me notes in class all morning on Thursday asking whether we were going out. Olivia Bush snapped a candid of us and blushingly asked whether she could use it for the yearbook. By lunch on Friday we laughed over what the rumor mill was saying. Zoë liked talk of our secret engagement. I preferred speculation that I was a religious zealot who had converted Jagger to join my cult.

Jagger, for his part, seemed eager for the exposure. He'd kissed me deeply again this morning. At my puzzled look when we came up for air, he'd admitted to liking the idea that the whole school knew he was mine.

"You didn't read it in *US Weekly?*" I asked in response to his paparazzi question. "I'm pregnant with your alien love child."

He laughed at that. "So I'm an alien now? That's a step up from yesterday. Cults kind of creep me out."

When we passed the two douches with the truck from the gas station, they were staring at Jagger and me. I resisted the urge to stick out my tongue. Zoë did not resist her urge to give them the finger.

We went our separate ways then, Zoë with Gunther to her place and I with Jagger to his. I'd been blissful all day, but my apprehension mounted as we approached his house. I was thrilled—and terrified—to meet his parents and spend time where he lived. I think he could tell I was nervous, which made him nervous, which made us both, well...nervous. I just hoped to hell my initial judgment of our worlds being too different turned out not to be true.

His house was modern and enormous, all light through glass and art. Yet, strangely, it felt like a home. Though I was certain that some of the paintings and trinkets I saw cost more than a brand new car, it seemed elegant rather than ostentatious and the design assembled to a perfect fit.

Grinning like a little boy as we approached the kitchen, he grabbed my hand to pull me forth.

"I smell cookies," he declared.

"Oatmeal chocolate chip?" I asked peering down at the delicious-looking biscuits on the plate.

He nodded reverent affirmation. Pulling back the Saran Wrap, he pinched off a corner of the biggest cookie and held it up to my lips. My eyes rolled back and I moaned a little as I tasted the exquisite confection.

"You shouldn't make sounds like that when I have you alone, Roxy. It's giving me ideas."

He was being playful, but his dark eyes and slightly strained voice made it clear that the words he was saying were true.

I've been having ideas all along, I wanted to say. But since I didn't want his parents' first impression to involve me getting jiggy with their son on their gorgeous granite countertop, I reined in my hormones and let him keep feeding us cookies.

"Thirsty?" he asked after we'd eaten half the plate.

"What do you have?" I asked casually, because casual had become my middle name. I was a study in exuding normalcy despite an inward state of perpetual bliss.

"Soda, purple stuff, Sunny D."

I chuckled. "How 'bout a glass of milk?"

By the time we resumed our tour of the downstairs, I was more at ease. When I laid eyes on the black Steinway in the music room, I smiled.

"Play for me?"

"Only if you sit next to me." I joined him on the bench.

What came next was the most hauntingly beautiful melody I couldn't help but feel I'd heard somewhere before. That I couldn't specifically remember when or where didn't stop me from begging him to keep playing. I vacillated between rapturous surrender to the music itself and shock that my dark, tortured man hid something so beautiful. I was dimly aware of the day fading to dusk, and how we were still sitting close in the dark. His foot on the pedal made the last of the notes linger. I felt loss when they faded away.

"Did you like it?" His whisper was insecure.

Under other circumstances I might have laughed, but such thoughts stopped when he lifted his eyes. What I saw in them matched the intensity of his song and swept me deeper into his ocean. Pulling his hands off of the keys, I brought one to my arm and ran his fingers across my goosebumps. I swallowed thickly, gathering my courage. Our faces were so close I could feel his breath.

"It's the most beautiful thing I've ever heard," I confessed, not realizing we weren't alone.

"It's the most beautiful thing he's ever written," came a wise, delicate voice that had to belong to his mother.

I barely had time to register my shock that Jagger had actually *composed* the masterpiece I just heard.

"Mom, this is my girlfriend, Roxy." He helped me off of the bench and as he spoke he smiled shyly and sounded proud. "Roxy, this is my mom," he gestured in between us as we crossed to where his mother stood.

"It's such a pleasure to meet you, Roxy," she exclaimed warmly, pulling me into a hug. "We're thrilled that you could come."

"It's nice to meet you, too, Mrs. Monroe," I said, still surprised at the gesture, even as we pulled away. "Thank you so much for having me."

By contrast to Jagger's taller build, she stood the same height as me and was a bit round in the middle. The green of her eyes was a darker shade than his sage-colored ones, and the burnt amber of her hair was brighter. But in their lips and their fore-heads they looked alike and, like Jagger, she was quite beautiful.

"Please, dear, call me Elsie. At home, we're pretty informal."

She was striking, but not intimidating. Refined, but approachable. And, just like her house, the contrast worked. She pulled my hand from Jagger's and hitched our arms as we climbed the stairs. She asked whether I was okay with pork chops for dinner and promised we'd be great friends.

"This must be Roxy!" the second most gorgeous man I had ever seen exclaimed, placing the lid on a pot and wiping his hands as we walked into the kitchen. He took my hand from Elsie and encased it in both of his, grasping them warmly in a light shake. "Welcome, Roxy. I'm Jagger's dad. Please call me Jack."

"It's a pleasure to meet you, Dr.—...Jack," I stammered with a blush.

"You didn't exaggerate, son," he beamed, shifting a proud gaze at Jagger. "She's absolutely charming."

"Dad..." Jagger said in a tone between a warning and a whine, but Jack ignored him and turned his attention back to me.

"We have a Beatles-only rule for dinnertime listening. Which would you prefer: *Revolver* or *Abbey Road*?"

"Do you have *The White Album*?" I asked, still shy. "That one's my favorite."

Jack smiled even more widely and placed a fatherly arm around me.

"Magnificent taste, my dear."

The hour that followed was a foray into something the likes of which I'd not witnessed before: a family sitting around the dinner table, laughing together, sharing a lovingly prepared meal. A single thought looped through my head like a mantra:

Do I really get to keep this?

I wanted to keep it all. The clique full of beautiful people. My doting boyfriend who showed me off and wrote beautiful songs. A cookie-baking mother who was better than mine. I wanted to be sure. And though his recent validation had carried me far, I still held the tiniest remnants of doubt.

Jagger had said all the right things and brought up some fair points when we'd finally talked. But he also dazzled me into kissing him before we really finished talking-the longer that sat with me, the less I liked it. If there really was a good explanation for my lingering questions (like, where did he disappear off to on Tuesdays and Thursdays, and why didn't anyone else seem to know? And what did he do to all those girls last year to make them hate him so much?) now would be the time to clue me in. Because I really wanted to keep this, and I needed affirmations that what I so dearly wanted could really be mine.

TWENTY-ONE
SAY YOU WON'T LET GO

I knew I loved you then,
but you'd never know
'cause I played it cool
when I was scared of letting go.
-James Arthur, *Say You Won't Let Go*

JAGGER

"I hope they didn't embarrass you too much," I whispered in Roxy's ear as we climbed the stairs.

Annika, Declan, Zoë and Gunther had just shown up, and we were all headed up to my room.

"For the record, I did not encourage my mother to take an interest in your shampoo-commercial hair or your flawless complexion...though I do agree with her on both counts."

She just smirked. "Any embarrassment I suffered at your parents' hands was worth the look on your face when the baby pictures came out. Wittle Jagger was so cuuuute!"

Her hand reached out to pinch my cheek, and Declan snickered loudly. I felt smug satisfaction when my reaching out to smack him earned a smirk from Annika.

"Besides," Roxy said, "we're even now. I owed you one after my dad."

Damn right you did, I thought indignantly as I squeezed my girl's hand.

Heedless of the others as we walked into my room, I watched for Roxy's reaction. Part of me was afraid she'd freak when she saw all my stuff. I could tell the house and the cars and all the antiques had given her pause. Relief washed over me when she scanned the room and smiled.

"Welcome to the bat cave," I said finally, ushering them all in. "Home to our Friday nights."

"Why do you call it "the bat cave"?" Zoë asked, flitting across the room, starting to check out all of my stuff.

"'Cause Bruce Wayne here is all dark and mysterious, and this place is like his *lair*."

Fucking Declan.

"I thought you guys just hung out and played video games." Annika eyed my monster computer set-up speculatively. "This place looks wired to initiate Def Con 5."

"Actually, Annika, Declan's quite fond of my computer..." I said suggestively.

Take that, fucker!

"I'm sure he'd be happy to give you a tour."

Turning away before I could catch the receiving end of Declan's death stare, I fixed my eyes back on my Roxy.

"Shall I kick your ass at Guitar Hero now?" I smiled wickedly.

"You can certainly try." Her smile was sweet.

An hour and a half later, we'd abandoned the video games and were paired off in various spots in the room: Declan and Annika on the couch, Zoë in Gunther's lap on the computer chair and Roxy and I propped up on our stomachs and elbows on the bed.

Yeah. I know.

Sick of Gunther and Deck handing me my ass about Roxy's epic Guitar Hero win, I changed the subject to what we'd be doing the following night.

"So what *is* roller derby, anyway?"

By then, I was the only non-initiate. Even Gunther had done his research. Annika and Zoë's team were up against Littleton and the rest of us were going to watch the bout.

"Soft porn," Declan mumbled reverently, which only earned him another smack.

"*Shut up.* It's a serious game." Annika turned to me then. "The object of the game is for one player on each team to score as many times as possible in a two minute period. That one player—the jammer—scores a point each time she can lap a group of blockers."

"Get to the good part, babe," Declan whined, "Tell him about *the names*."

My interest was piqued when Gunther chuckled. Even Roxy was laughing.

The names?

Gunther pointed at Zoë and Annika.

"When you hear "Zobra Kai" and "Anita Reason" called onto the rink, the announcer is talking about *them*."

By the time they were on about the finer points of the game I had completely lost interest. I blamed Roxy, who was curled next to me in the most appealing way as she scrolled through the music on my phone.

"What are we listening to next?"

I rested my head on her shoulder and kissed under her ear.

"I like the songs on this one playlist called 'Beautiful'," she said.

Her perfect oblivion as she went through the business of scrolling through made me just *have to* say what I said next.

"You should," I admitted so that only she could hear. "Those songs make me think of you. That's how I came up with the playlist name. *Roxy. Beautiful.*"

Her finger stilled on the iPod and I felt her take a deep breath.

"Why do you say things like that?" she whispered, sliding her deep brown eyes up to mine.

"I only say what I feel."

Gone were the days of me hiding how I felt. She was giving me a look like she gave me when I'd played for her. I hoped I was right about what I thought it meant.

"What do you feel right now?" she asked as if torn between wanting and not wanting the answer.

I love you. Some part of me knew it all along.

"The first time I say it, I want us to be alone."

Please, love me back, Roxy.

"Me too."

My lip twitched before curling into a disbelieving smile, one that quickly turned into a grin. And then she was smiling too and I was showering her with kisses and rolling her playfully on my bed.

"Get a room, you two!" Gunther shouted jokingly, but he was smiling as he looked over.

Roxy and I were both laughing as I pulled her into my arms.

"This *is* my fucking room."

———

ROXY

"So give me the scoop—how was meeting his parents?" Zoë asked excitedly as we sped away in her car.

"It was perfect," I sighed dreamily. "Everything was perfect."
And it really felt like it was.

"Well I think I might need a new doctor," she said, looking
like she wasn't joking. "Did you see Dr. Monroe?"

"Oh my God, Zoë..."

"Whatever." she huffed. "I'm not blind."

Zoë chattered on about how she wouldn't mind getting a
physical from Jack and how Jagger would look like him one day. I
was only partially listening, my mind consumed with something
else. Meeting his parents? Hanging out in his room? A triple-date,
for cripe's sake? We were joined in ways I'd have laughed at two
weeks ago. The chemistry between us was insane, and the
emotion was becoming too great.

"Things looked pretty cozy with you and Gunther," I fished
carefully. "How are things going with that?"

Her eyes really should have been on the road, for how fast
she was going, but she trained a knowing gaze on me.

"You mean, when are we going to do the deed?" she asked
cheekily. "He's sleeping over tomorrow night. Being the child of
neglectful parents has its merits and Niede won't tell."

Sometimes I worried about Zoë, wondered if her wild-child
tendencies were a twisted cry for help. I got the sense Gunther
pulled her out of some of her shit and gave her love and attention
no one ever had. She hid it well, but Zoë's life was not ideal.

"Jagger and I are...getting closer." I mumbled.

"No shit," Zoë laughed. "You can't keep your hands off of each
other, and that boy is in love. If I wasn't sure you felt the same
way, I'd warn you to be careful with his heart."

For the most part, her eyes were back on the road, but she
took a long moment to cast a smug glance.

"Looks like all's well that ends well," she murmured quietly.

Or, translated into Zoë-speak: *I told you so.*

JAGGER

I watched Roxy's ass appreciatively as she sauntered to the snack bar. She was wearing those tight jeans again. Her shiny hair cascaded in waves down her back and a snug, long-sleeved v-neck hugged her delicious curves.

"Looks like all's well that ends well, huh, bro?"

Declan had caught me staring. He'd torn himself away from his own girlfriend's ass long enough to throw me a shit-eating grin.

"No need to thank me now," he continued in a low, hoarse voice, "but some day, and that day may never come, I'll call upon you to do a service for me. But until that day – accept this justice as a gift on my daughter's wedding day."

I blinked.

"Declan. What the *fuck* are you talking about?"

He took a little step back in surprise.

"Please tell me you've seen *The Godfather*."

Seriously. What the hell was he talking about? When I looked distractedly at Roxy again, he laughed.

"I'm saying *you're welcome*. You're happier than a pig in shit since you got with Roxy. And, see? Your boy had your back. We both know you never would have friended her yourself."

Jesus. I'd been so love-drunk these past couple of weeks that I'd forgotten to do cleanup on how it all began. I'd intended to ask Deck and Gunther after my date with Roxy in Littleton to corroborate my story if anyone ever asked. But I'd forgotten and here we were, and I had to make sure he understood.

"She can never find out the truth."

My voice held equal parts determination and fear. Things with us were still new and we were on the verge of something wonderful. Hearing it could make her doubt everything.

"What's the big deal, man?" Declan frowned. "It's kind of a funny story. Roxy would understand."

"Roxy would understand?" I mimicked incredulously, "I guess since women are so understanding all of a sudden, I can tell Annika what she'll find if she looks in the second spare tire bay in the back of your Jeep. I'm sure she'd be particularly interested in your fetish for electrical ass fucking and your membership to Sexy Preggo Sluts."

"That's fucked up," Declan scowled before casting a guilty glance toward where a ferocious-looking Annika took no prisoners as she played the game.

"I know," I admitted, "but I want Roxy to like me. And this is one in a small but lethal handful of secrets she is not allowed to know. If she asks you, lie. I'm serious, man. She can never find out the truth."

Declan looked back at me and nodded his acquiescence.

"Too late," Roxy's angry, hurt voice growled at my back.

Please, no.

I closed my eyes and pinched the bridge of my nose.

"Roxy," I began, turning to face her, but all I saw was her back. She was already walking away.

PART THREE

TOTAL ECLIPSE OF THE HEART

TWENTY-TWO

DAUGHTERS

Fathers, be good to your daughters.
Daughters will love like you do.
Girls become lovers who turn into mothers.
So, mothers be good to your daughters, too.
-John Mayer, *Daughters*

LUCAS VEGA

"Breakfast, Roxx?"

I poked my head into her room and saw that she was still in bed.

"I thought we'd go to the di—"

Taking in my daughter's wide, unfocused eyes, I stopped short. She looked awake, but not really there. My adrenaline surged.

"What happened?" My voice was authoritative and alarmed.

Her eyes were eerily blank as she looked up at me.

"Did somebody hurt you?" I struggled to keep my calm.

That seemed to snap her out of it, because suddenly her eyes were sharp.

"What? No, Dad. Just...no."

Her quick reaction—an intuitive one—caused me to believe her.

"I think Jagger and I broke up," she whispered miserably.

Kids and their whirlwind romances. He only took her to that concert two weeks ago...

Taking a seat on the edge of her bed, I stayed with her in silence. Having recently bought a book about being a single father to a teenage girl, I knew there was a chance she'd want to "talk".

"You think, but you're not sure?"

She sniffled miserably.

"Technically, I never said the words."

So it was she *who broke up with* him. *Good.*

She sat up a little and fixed me with searching eyes.

"If a girl just kept walking away, even if you were calling after her, would you think you were broken up?"

Attagirl, Roxx! I concealed a smile.

"That would depend on what I'd done."

She held a tissue in her hand, one that her fingers had started to shred.

"He lied to me, Dad."

Then she launched into a lengthy story. To tell you the God's honest truth, what they were fighting about sounded like the stupidest thing I'd ever heard. But I thought of the parenting book and how I was supposed to be supportive and remember that I, too, had been a teenager once.

"Give yourself some time, Roxx. If he's worth his salt, he'll wait as long as it takes."

I reached to the back of her head and tousled her hair. Her answering smile was sad but grateful. Before letting me leave she'd made me promise to run interference on all of her visits and calls.

Ten minutes later I was walking out the door to head to the diner alone. I was thinking about whether to bring Roxy back pancakes or waffles to cheer her up when I tripped over something large.

What the hell?

My gaze shot to my feet. Jagger Monroe and his crazy hair were sleeping on my porch.

Not so much sleeping anymore.

The kid had startled awake. For a brief moment, he was bewildered. I saw the moment recollection set in. I almost felt bad for the guy for how quickly his face fell, but I was on Roxy's side.

"Mr. Vega, good morning."

I got the sense that Jagger was well-mannered, even when he wasn't kissing my ass. I wouldn't go so far as to say that I liked the kid, but I liked that my daughter liked him, at least until last night. She was barely seventeen, but her judgement of character had always been good.

"Morning, Jagger. I know why you're here. But, I'm sorry—she's asked not to see you. Now, that's what she said, but this part is from me: Do not. Lie. To my daughter."

He looked deeply ashamed as he scrambled to his feet. I saw the moment his gaze swept over my utility knife, the instant he recalled our talk from the week before.

"Now, you're gonna leave and I'm going out to get breakfast and you're gonna give my daughter some time."

Something more flashed in his eyes—this time, resolve.

"With all due respect, sir, I'd like to stay. I doubt that my word means much to her right now, so I'd like my presence to speak for how much I care."

Holy hell.

The kid loved Roxy. I could see it in his eyes. He reminded me of a young me.

"And, sir? I can guarantee you that I will never lie to Roxy again and that lying last night was the stupidest thing I've ever done."

I sighed and scrubbed my fingers over my beard. I'd been in the doghouse with a woman enough times to want to give him a chance.

"I appreciate that, but I have to respect Roxy's wishes. I'll be sure to tell her you were here."

Continuing down the steps and hoping to effectively end the conversation, I listened for his steps behind me. His feet didn't move and instead I got his voice, steady and strong.

"I know you've been in love before, Mr. Vega. What I mean is, I know you and Roxy's mother were once in love. Only love could create a person as special as Roxy."

My feet stopped moving and I turned back to look at him again. *This kid is good.*

"Well, I'm in love with your daughter. And I mean no disrespect to you or her, sir. I only mean to fix it."

The thing was, I could smell bullshit from miles away, and he was sincere.

"I left a message on her phone asking her to come out and talk to me. If she doesn't, I swear I'll leave her alone. No throwing stones at her window. I'll let her come to me."

I didn't have the heart to tell him she was stubborn like her mother. Both of them could brood for days. Taking pity on him, I nodded and looked down at my feet. I didn't want the kid to starve. He looked pretty beat down and could probably use some breakfast.

"How do you like your eggs?"

TWENTY-THREE

SUPERMAN (IT'S NOT EASY)

It may sound absurd, but don't be naive
Even heroes have the right to bleed.
I may be disturbed, but won't you concede
Even heroes have the right to dream.
-Five for Fighting, *Superman* (*It's Not Easy*)

JAGGER

I wasn't sure Mr. Vega liked me, but I no longer suspected he wished me dead. He had brought me breakfast and coffee and left the front door open so I could use the small bathroom in the hall. By Sunday evening, the Vega porch had hosted a revolving door of visitors. Friends and family brought reinforcements and the occasional word of advice.

Declan was the first, and I was unspeakably happy to see him. Aside from my transgression against Roxy, what I'd asked of Declan had been out of line. I apologized for being a dick and using what I knew about his "recreational activities" as leverage, assuring him I'd said all of it not out of intention, but fear. He accepted the apology with grace, and sat with me awhile in silent solidarity because that's the kind of friend Declan was.

Zoë was next. I suspected that if she hadn't found me there by coincidence, she might have paid me a visit of her own.

"I know why you did what you did," she announced, as she marched up the front steps. I had nearly a foot on her, but she got right in my face. "But if you ever lie to Roxy again, you'll be shitting teeth."

After holding one of the most threatening glares that had been leveled at me in...well, ever, she continued on inside without another word. I was still a little spooked when she came out a moment later. I raised an eyebrow in surprise. I'd thought she would be in there for hours.

"Looks like Roxy won't see either of us." I could see the hurt through her pride.

Before I could think up a response, she flipped her chin toward the gray fleece blanket I always kept in the trunk of my car.

"What's that?"

I looked at the blanket, then back at her.

"It's what I slept under last night."

She nodded approvingly, her gray eyes twinkling as she got set to leave. A second before she disappeared into her car, she called two words and smiled.

"Carry on."

My mother was next. I'd explained where I was on the phone the night before. When I hadn't returned by noon she'd called ahead to find out what I wanted for lunch. I placed a tall order that involved a basket of supplies and made an afterthought out of the food. We'd split one of the three BLTs she brought (go overboard much, Mom?) and a thermos of hot cider while sitting on the porch step.

After years of practice, she knew not to fuss or hound. She

could tell that I was beating myself up enough for everyone, and spared her admonitions. In knowing her as well, I correctly anticipated that she wouldn't leave without imparting a kernel of wisdom.

"God brings men into deep water, not to drown them but to cleanse them," she whispered in my ear as I hugged her goodbye.

For the next hour, I sat with the guitar-monogrammed note cards and letter paper my mother had brought me from home. God bless that woman for thinking of the little stuff. As I began squeezing fathoms of my feelings onto the small canvas I had to work with, I concluded that the written word was an apt hedge for whatever else might fly from my mouth.

I heard the engine of Gunther's '65 Mustang from half a mile down the road. He drove it so seldom, any other day I'd hop up at the chance to admire his flawless restoration. But he looked troubled as he emerged from his car. He cast a grim glance toward Roxy's window before crossing her front lawn slowly, his attention focused upward for a long moment before catching my eyes.

"It's not about what happened last night. You know that, right?"

I blinked. "Then what is it about?"

"That's easy, dude—she's scared."

He sat down, and I felt a little bit better, somehow more open and calm. I let him talk, not above accepting help. He was comically dense when it came to Zoë, but when it came to figuring out everyone else's shit, Gunther was pretty wise.

"Love and hate are parallel emotions, just like anger and fear. No one was ever angry who wasn't afraid of something."

I thought of my anger with Declan the night before.

"What if I don't have the slightest idea what she's afraid of?"

"You may not, dude. You haven't even been together two weeks. Besides, it's not like you can read minds."

Fucking right I can't.

"Yeah, especially not Roxy's."

Gunther started playing with a blade of grass.

"Look, dude. I can't say too much. But a mini-version of this happened with Zoë. She's got a bunch of baggage that has nothing to do with me. It made her push me away. Zoë moves at ludicrous speed, so at least she gets over shit quick. But Roxy's different—less decisive. She takes her time. I'm sure you know that by now."

I looked up at her window. I did know that.

We fist-bumped and he climbed into his car. I watched it disappear down the street. The more I thought about what he'd said, the more I realized he had to be right. Hadn't Roxy and I bonded over our taste in maudlin music? Hadn't what drew me to her always been the knowledge of a certain darkness we shared? This girl had demons, and I'd triggered something big. I only hoped she'd take me back and one day I'd find out what.

"Are you sure she's worth it?" Annika asked without preamble, settling next to me on the step.

By the time she came, the sun was setting and I was a few hours shy of twenty-four.

I nodded with conviction. "She's like us, but she's not like us. She's been hurt and abandoned before. And she doesn't have what we have, Annika. It's just her and her dad. Before me, Zoë was her only real friend."

She nodded in a way that I knew meant she understood. Annika knew what it was to be alone.

"All I care about is that she doesn't hurt and abandon *you*."

I wrapped my arm around her and squeezed.

"I know."

———

I WAS FORCED to leave Roxy's against my will. Though Mr. Vega had become sympathetic to my cause, I'd slept at his house for two nights with no success. Beyond that, I was still a teenage boy trying to get close to his daughter, so it was no surprise he'd given me the boot.

Now I was in school, and I was miserable. Roxy wasn't here. My classes moved too slowly and my obsessive Instagram stalking didn't help pass the time. By then, I'd let go of absurd fantasies of a happy reunion. I just wanted to know my girl was okay.

By lunchtime, I had received no such comfort. Even worse, I'd had to endure what seemed like dozens of imbecilic updates. Dutton posted a "Looks like someone's got a case of the Mondays" meme. Olivia Bush sent out a post reminding folks to vote for a theme for Jr. Prom—a prom I'd been building up to ask Roxy to before I'd screwed up. I briefly considered unfriending every single person I knew except for Roxy. But if I did that, I couldn't troll their walls. Professional Instagram stalker that I was, I couldn't pass up the chance to spy on her through her friends. Speaking of things inquiring minds had no right to know...

"Dude, I heard you and Roxy broke up."

What the fuck?

Glaring up at the voice that had interrupted me from Instagram, I came face to face with Dan Wesley. I didn't know why he was talking to me about my girl but I knew immediately I didn't like it.

"What?" I snapped.

He seemed oblivious to my tone.

"I heard you tapped that ass! I know she plays all innocent, but—" he looked around conspiratorially before lowering his voice and leaning in, "—man to man, does she like it rough?"

I was up in a second. And a second after that, his neck was in my hand. Three seconds after that I'd strode us both across the room and pinned him to the nearest wall.

"What the *fuck* did you just say about my girlfriend?"

That I had never been in a fight did not stop me from drilling my fist into his face. Once was not enough, apparently. At least that's what I was told later. I'd been so blind with rage, I remembered almost nothing, even after I'd been pulled off. At some point, I realized I was being shaken. Looking up, I saw the concerned face of my dad.

Seeing beyond where he was crouched in front of me, I realized where I was sitting: with my back against the brick wall of the cafeteria. I dimly wondered how long I'd been there. Then I wondered how long my dad had been there.

"Does it hurt?"

I shook my head, because it didn't. I was numb, and not from the cold.

"C'mon." He jutted his chin toward the visitor parking lot. "I'll take you home."

He helped me up, brushed me off a little, and clapped his hand on my shoulder. A minute later, we were speeding toward my house. For the first time since Saturday, my mind was quiet, almost like I wasn't even there. The warmth of the seat heat opposed the cool window against my temple. The hum of the engine gave me a foreign sense of peace. The color of the evergreens as we whipped past them was beautiful. I felt as if I could go to sleep.

"They gave you a three-day suspension for fighting in school." His voice was calm. "You know, you broke Dan Wesley's nose."

Because the suspension didn't surprise me and I felt no remorse, I kept staring out the window and said nothing.

"Do you know what he said?" I asked my dad minutes later as we sat silently in the car. The Mercedes was in the garage, the engine was cut and I hadn't moved an inch. "He asked when he could fuck Roxy now that I was done with her and wanted to know whether she liked it rough."

The next thing out of my dad's mouth reminded me why I loved him so much.

"Sounds like he had it coming."

TWENTY-FOUR

APOLOGIZE

I'm holdin' on a rope,
got me ten feet off the ground.
I'm hearing what you say
but I just can't make a sound.
-One Republic, *Apologize*

ROXY

"Da-aad," I whined as I felt the nudge on my shoulder, "Lemme sleep. I'm still not up to going to school."

I buried my head under the pillow and pulled the covers up, but the nudging didn't stop.

"I'm serious, Dad," I groused irritably, wishing he would continue to let me wallow. "I got my period last night and my cramps are really bad."

Menstrual talk was like kryptonite to him. But if I didn't play my trump card, he'd make me go to school.

"Your dad left for work five minutes ago, Roxy, which means he's not here to protect you from *me*."

Second on the list of people I wasn't ready to face was Zoë.

"Get up," she hissed viciously at the same time she ripped off all my covers.

Please, God. Just kill me now.

I turned to glare at her. "Did you stake out my house and break into the back door, or did my dad actually let you in?"

Her glare was better.

"Neither. I used the spare key in the mailbox. As your *best friend* I knew where it was."

I winced. At the time, it had seemed fitting to extend my visitor ban to include Zoë. Hers was the only call I'd answered on Saturday, the day after roller derby. The way she'd immediately started defending him told me she'd already picked her side.

"About that—" I started, but she cut me off.

Maybe it was time to extend the olive branch. It still irked me that she'd been so quick to defend Jagger, but I missed her and I needed a friend.

"No, Roxy. You go dark for three days? You can go dark for one day longer. And we'll get back to what kind of friend you've been to me in due time. For now I'm your fairy godmother."

I shut up, mainly because Zoë was scaring me, but also because I was losing my fight. The quick change of heart pretty much summed up my last couple days: I was a schizophrenic mess. By now I could admit it was stupid for me to be pissed about Declan being the one to friend me—but what about Jagger's lies? If he'd go to such lengths to hide something I'd forgive, he had to be hiding more.

And he was, wasn't he?

Damn skippy he was. He'd said as much himself: "lethal" secrets about which I "could never find out the truth". When Zoë asked again why I couldn't forgive him, I'd be pointing straight to that.

But my heart knew a deeper truth: I'd been waiting for the

ship to hit the iceberg. And as soon as it did, like a coward, I'd jumped the first lifeboat out.

Women and children first.

And that was my problem. I had always made like we were the *Titanic*—the most splendid thing to ever sail the northern seas, but destined somehow to sink. And I was one of the skeptics who'd gone aboard, all the while believing it was too good to be true.

Why couldn't you believe you deserved all of him, Roxy?

That question, above all others, was what kept me catatonic. I rarely cried, but these past few days I'd wept buckets. I knew I wasn't dynamic like Zoë or confident like Annika. But I'd thought I had a little more self-esteem.

Don't go there.

But I *had* gone there, a dozen times in as many hours. I'd finally figured out why a relationship with Jagger paralyzed me with fear. My naïve mother never learned not to believe every single lie all those rich, handsome, only-after-one-thing sugar daddies told her, and I couldn't end up like my mother.

"I'm not taking you to class. There are things you need to see. Resistance would be futile, understand?"

I nodded dumbly.

"Good. Now, take a shower and put something decent on. You have enough problems. The last thing you need is to be seen looking like that."

A quick glance in the mirror revealed tear-tracks on my face and bird's nest hair. When I returned from the shower, I saw that Zoë had tidied my room and put fresh sheets on my bed. It made me feel even worse for shutting her out.

"Zoë...just, thanks." She gave me a look that was intended to give warning but I could see she was fighting to stay mad.

She shook her head then, but her face softened.

"Don't thank me just yet. It's only been three days, but you have missed a *lot*."

I took her exit as my cue to follow. I felt weak as I descended the stairs and found I couldn't remember the last time I had eaten. I started toward the kitchen but she pulled me into the dining room, where I was assaulted by a sweet smell. The table held three bouquets of exotic flowers that looked like ones I'd seen in Mrs. Monroe's garden. I blinked in disbelief.

"This is the gift table, Roxy. It has everything Jagger sent to the house since Saturday night. There's more on the other side."

I circled the table slowly, and sure enough there was another pile of stuff—the green iPod Shuffle and a white Nano I'd never seen. There were cards—lots of them.

"Start reading," Zoë commanded gently.

I pulled out a flat note card in the same fine stock as the envelope. It held the motif of a guitar.

> *How can I just let you walk away,*
> *just let you leave without a trace,*
> *when I stand here taking every*
> *breath with you? You're the only*
> *one who really knew me at all.*
> -Phil Collins
> *I won't walk away from you, Roxy. Please don't*
> *walk away from me.*

Song lyrics. Jagger was sending me song lyrics, knowing how they would get to me.

"Keep reading, Roxy. There're a dozen more."

I reached to pull out the chair at my hip and lowered myself to sit on wobbly legs. My hand shook as I retrieved the second card.

Some people want it all,
but I don't want nothing at all
if it ain't you baby,
if I ain't got you baby.
-Alicia Keys
Roxy, I'm not giving up on us. I'll do whatever
    it takes.

Looking up at Zoë, I shook my head, unsure that I could continue. She only handed me a third.

We belong to the light,
we belong to the thunder.
We belong to the sound of the
words we've both fallen under.
Whatever we deny or embrace,
for worse or for better.
We belong, we belong,
we belong together.
-Pat Benatar
Please, Roxy. Let me apologize. I'm nothing
    without you.

I heard the sniffle, but I didn't realize it had come from me. Didn't know my tears were falling until one landed on the note.

"I can't do this." My voice sounded small.

This time the hand she held out contained a tissue. "You *can* and you *will.*"

She'd handed me five tissues by the time I read through the pile, which seemed to contain lyrics from every epic love song that had ever topped the charts.

"C'mon," she tugged at my elbow. "We'll listen to the playlists in my car. Right now we have some place to go."

She placed the rest of the items into her purse and we headed out the front door. I nearly tripped over a blanket I recognized—the gray blanket Jagger had wrapped us in as we'd spent that magical afternoon by the seaside bluff.

What the hell?

Zoë gave me a pointed look.

"That's the blanket Jagger shivered under the two nights he spent sleeping on your porch."

I had to swallow a couple of times before my voice worked.

"Jagger slept here?"

She didn't need to answer. Instead, she just led me to her car. Things got worse when she docked the Nano and started playing his songs. Ten minutes later I sat, dejected and remorseful with my head against the window, drowning in the Mariah Carey version of *We Belong Together* when the jolt of the car pulling into somewhere caused me to open my eyes.

"I thought we weren't going to school," I whined pathetically.

"I said we weren't going to class," Zoë clarified. "It's 9:45. Second period started ten minutes ago. No one will be in the halls."

I felt like a loser when I tried, and failed, at not scanning the parking lot for his car.

"He's not here."

Where is he? I wouldn't let myself ask.

"He got a three-day suspension."

By then we were climbing the steps to the school building, and I stopped short.

"Suspended! For what?"

"Breaking Dan Wesley's jaw."

She grabbed my elbow to drag me forward and I was too bewildered to protest.

"Jagger was fighting?"

She turned to pin me with another powerful look. "Jagger was fighting for *you*."

"I don't' understand." I shook my head, unseeing as I followed Zoë down the hall. "What does some kid named Dan Wesley have to do with me?"

"He wasn't kind enough to introduce himself to you at the gas station that morning." she said bitterly. "He heard you and Jag broke up and said some pretty crass things. It took Declan and two teachers to pull him off."

Jagger defended me.

"Is he okay?" I nearly shouted, panic lacing my voice.

Zoë reached into her purse and pulled out her phone.

"Maybe you should ask him yourself."

I shook my head immediately. I wasn't ready.

Zoë huffed and shook her head, looking off to the side in frustration. "Physically, he's fine."

I followed her mutely as she walked us into the building. Jagger had a reputation for a lot of things, but fighting wasn't one of them. Were the permanent records grown-ups talked about real, and would a three-day suspension go on Jagger's?

"We're here."

I stopped walking when she did. It was then that I realized we were at my locker. Only it didn't look like my locker. It looked like some kind of shrine. More of the same guitar-embossed cards bearing Jagger's handwriting had been taped on front, this time without the envelopes. They all held lyrics to more songs.

What do you think I would
give at this moment?
If you'd stay I'd subtract twenty
years from my life.
I'd fall down on my knees,
kiss the ground that you walk on,

If I could just hold you again.
-Billy Vera
Please take me back, Roxy.

I couldn't believe my eyes. Five similar cards with equally apologetic song lyrics were taped down my locker in artistic formation for all the world to see.

For all the world to see.

The tears—tears of guilt this time—started once again.

What have I done?

TWENTY-FIVE
LOVER YOU SHOULD'VE COME OVER

Maybe I'm too young
to keep good love from going wrong.
But tonight, you're on my mind,
so you'll never know.
-Jeff Buckley, *Lover You Should've Come Over*

ZOË

After she'd seen what I needed her to see at school, I took Roxy to my house. I couldn't risk her kicking me out of hers. As hurt as part of me was by her behavior, the larger part had seen it coming. All along, she'd been waiting for the other shoe to drop. Only, she didn't seem to realize she'd practically thrown it.

Gunther: How's Operation "Head-Out-of-Your-Ass" coming along?

Gunther was texting me surreptitiously from study hall. I glanced over to where Roxy sat on my bed, surrounded by tissues, awash in silent tears.

Zoë: She's taking it pretty hard. Is Operation "Pull-Yourself-Together-Man" faring any better?

Gunther: Not even close. He's not answering his phone, but I know he's still alive.

Zoë: Let me guess. Instagram?

Gunther: I think he's hoping she'll log on.

Zoë: That's on this afternoon's agenda. Maybe that will end this?

Gunther: I hope so, Sugar. Call me when you're done. Love you.

Zoë: I love you too, babe.

Forty-five minutes and half a box of tissues later, Roxy was still rereading his letters, still mopping her eyes and sniffling when I got up from my desk chair and sat next to her on my bed.

"If this is how he feels, why did he lie?"

They were the first words she had spoken to me since we left the school.

"You scared him, Roxx." My voice was gentle, but firm. I had to give her tough love. "And based on the way you *completely overreacted*, he had you all figured out."

She sniffled. "What's that supposed to mean? And why are you making excuses for him—again?"

"I'm not," I insisted. "And I think it's interesting how you haven't mentioned that, technically, *I* accepted his friend request."

She had the decency to look chagrined.

"I'll ignore the irony of that and focus on the real issue."

"And what is the real issue?" she mocked without much fight.

"You were skeptical all along. He knew it, and it made him feel like he had something to prove."

She opened her mouth to protest, but I wouldn't let her get a word in.

"And I know how he feels. When we first met, you did the same exact thing to me."

Her mouth snapped shut.

"I'm not blind, Roxy. I know I drive a Porsche and you don't have your own car. I know the fact that I have a housekeeper makes you uncomfortable. I know I can roller skate backwards with both eyes closed while anything faster than a stroll makes you trip over your own feet. But here's the difference between us: *you care about those things.* And, at the beginning, you never let me forget it."

Her look of bewilderment told me I was getting through to her.

"You judged him the entire time, and it made him insecure. But he fell in love with you so hard that he'd have done anything it took to keep you. Even if 'anything' meant that he had to lie."

She looked away from me, out my window toward the darkening woods and overcast sky.

"All couples fight, Roxy. But the ones that survive talk things through. Don't turn this into more than it needs to be."

She looked partially convinced—I took that as a good sign. I had more ammo, but wasn't sure how much she could take.

"You stay here for awhile, maybe get some rest. I'll ask Neide to fix you soup." I offered, deciding against pushing too hard. "You haven't eaten all day, and you'll need strength for what's next."

———

ANNIKA

"Wake up," I growled in my most menacing voice which was, if I do say so myself, pretty menacing.

Roxy's face was mostly covered with a messy tangle of hair, and she opened one groggy, unfocused eye. She closed it a second later, appearing to go back to sleep. I scanned Zoë's bedroom for something heavy to throw, but Roxy shot up abruptly, looking utterly and completely afraid.

"Annika?"

I sneered. The veil of sleep began to lift, freeing her from her haze.

"You have five minutes to get downstairs and meet me in my car. We have a long drive."

She nodded shallowly, eyes still wide as I turned on my heel. She made it to my car with a minute to spare.

"Lunch," I declared, motioning to the thermos of soup that sat in the drink holder. I threw her a baggie of oyster crackers that she barely caught. How Zoë had presumed for somebody so uncoordinated to eat soup in a moving vehicle was beyond me. All I knew was that she'd better not spill any in my car.

"Is this another fairy godmother mission?" Roxy asked timidly as we sped out of town.

I smirked at Zoë's name for all this.

"Couldn't you tell by my costume? I'm Glinda, the Good Witch of the North."

Her eyes widened slightly as she held me in her regard, but she soon trained them back to the road ahead. *A Christmas Carol* would be more accurate—you know, if it were Christmas. Zoë had been the Ghost of Christmas Present and I'd be the Ghost of Christmas Past. We rode in silence: me, Roxy, and our pain. I sensed hers, but I doubted she sensed mine. I could count on one hand the people for whom I would reveal this, my deepest secret. I was doing this for Jagger—dear friend, confidante and the only one who understood. He loved her, and her position in his care-fully-guarded inner circle automatically placed her in mine.

At some point, she did manage a few crackers and a bit of her soup, but I could tell our mystery field trip had her spooked. When we were a few minutes away from our destination, I started talking. I looked as primped and put-together as I usually did, but inside I was in knots.

"You haven't been here long enough to remember Bryce

King. He and I dated all through freshman year. He was my first boyfriend—gorgeous, popular...the whole nine. I was in love with him. So much so, that I only saw what I wanted to see."

"I know the feeling..." she muttered, all bitter sadness.

"Shut up," I snarled. "You don't know anything. He did a lot worse than tell me one white lie."

She didn't know better. Still, I was livid that anyone would compare Jagger to Bryce.

This is exactly why we're doing this, I thought with simmering rage. *Someone needs to school this sanctimonious little...*

I forced myself to breathe.

"*As I was saying...*I ignored the signs that he wasn't a good guy. I let all the controlling and bad behavior when he was drinking and excuse-making slide because he always apologized and there were times when he was really sweet."

When I heard my breath shudder, I realized I was trembling.

"Then things got physical," I ground out.

I had her attention now.

"I deluded myself into thinking things were fine because I could usually find one of his friends to handle him when he got too rowdy at parties. This one night, I needed help and no one was around.

Roxy was so engrossed in what I was saying, she didn't notice we'd pulled off of the road and driven through wrought iron gates.

"That was how I ended up here."

She looked around, up at the canopy of trees that arched above the road, down the long driveway, and toward the chateau-style buildings that stood at the end.

"Where are we?" She'd missed the sign at the gate.

"The Sisters of the Holy Family."

Understanding dawned in her eyes.

"Hard to believe that they still have convents. Not only that—it turns out they're still dumping grounds for pregnant teens."

Roxy shook her head, no longer stuck in her own misery. For the moment, she was concerned with mine.

"I don't know what to say."

I was surprised when tears prickled my eyes, and more surprised still when I realized they were for her.

"You don't have to say anything. Just listen, okay? What I'm showing you today is really important."

Parking in front of the schoolhouse, I cut the engine and we got out of the car. The residence was beautiful; a large, turreted hall was the centerpiece of the stone structure. We walked up a grand staircase to the main landing, all shining wood floors anchored by an enormous fireplace. Identical staircases leading to yet another level above flanked opposite sides of curved walls. This place held some of the most painful memories of my life. It also held some of the most precious. In so many ways, this convent felt like home.

I walked us up the stairs to the third level, then up one more flight to the fourth. School was in session so the residence was empty. Our destination was my favorite window seat. It had everything a good window seat should. Soft, cushy pillows, room for two and an amazing view of the lake. I would start with my second story—the one with the happy ending. Roxy waited for me to begin.

"Once a week, the nuns would take us into town to do our shopping. One Saturday in June I ran into Declan. He was picking up prescriptions for his grandma, who lives, like, ten miles from here. Mind you, we had never been friends at school before. The school had been told I was in France on foreign exchange. I'd even missed the spring semester. Yet, there I was, 30 weeks pregnant, running into Declan while buying stretch mark cream and Preparation H.

"I panicked—like, started having an actual panic attack. I dropped everything in my hands. Every fear I had about people knowing what had happened to me came crashing down and I just...lost it. I still don't remember the whole episode. Somehow we made it out of the pharmacy and ended up on a sidewalk bench.

"I came to in his arms. When I realized what happened, I tried to get up and leave, but he only held me tighter. He held me like that 'til I had to go find the other girls and get my ride back to the convent. Before he put me in the van, he kissed my forehead and told me it would be okay."

"I spent the next week in tears, partially because seeing him like that made it all feel more real, but also because I was so heartbroken by his kindness. My parents had basically abandoned me here, convinced me that the rape was my fault, and hidden the pregnancy even from my brothers. They were forcing me to give my baby up for adoption, and they expected me to come home at the end of the summer and play like I'd been on exchange. Declan's humanity was the best thing that had happened to me in months and it kind of made me fall apart."

Roxy looked thoughtful as I let the information sink in. I'd seen her wince when I'd referred to the rape.

"I'm sorry all that happened to you, Annika," she said finally.

"Me, too. But it brought me to Declan. That next week, he showed up on visitors' day with a big bouquet of daisies. Said I was probably sick of people bringing me roses."

We shared our first real smile.

"He came to see me every week after that. Each visit, we sat right here in this spot. He felt the baby kick and rubbed my feet. He listened to my whole story and held me while I cried. He stood up to my parents and made them press charges against Bryce, but not before he kicked his ass. He told my brothers the truth and brought them to come see me." I teared up again at the memory. "I'd never been so happy to see those clowns in my life."

In her sorry state, Roxy was deep in tissues. She handed me one and we both swiped at our eyes.

"So here's the lesson, Roxy. There are good guys and bad guys, and I found out the difference the hard way. Jagger is one of the good ones—the kind you hold onto with all you've got. So he did something stupid, but guys are dumb like that. If you ever find yourself in a relationship with a guy who doesn't do stupid things, be afraid...

"And, don't think for a second I'm blind to Declan's faults just because he came to my rescue. I know all about his cage fighting addiction and all that kinky porn—why do you think he's so into pregnant chicks?"

Her jaw dropped in shock.

"Jagger's only human and good people do bad things. I can guarantee that you will regret not forgiving him."

She took a deep, stuttering breath, looking clearer than she had been when I'd picked her up that morning. "I know, I just...I wish I understood why."

"You two have only been dating for, like, two weeks Roxy. You can't expect him to lay it all down now. These things that happened with Declan took almost three months. And Jagger has his own share of junk."

She sniffled and nodded again. "Can I ask you a question? I mean, I know I'm supposed to be listening, but..."

What happened to your baby? I was sure it was coming.

"How do you know all this stuff about Jagger?"

TWENTY-SIX
NEED YOU NOW

It's a quarter after one,
I'm all alone and I need you now.
Said I wouldn't call but I
lost all control and I need you now.
-Lady Antebellum, *Need You Now*

ROXY

Annika had thrown a cryptic "You'll find out when we get back to Rye" as a non-answer to my only question. She'd gone beyond defending Jagger—she'd spoken of him with a certain reverence. Before, I'd assumed their only association was their common link: Declan. If I hadn't just heard how deep things were between she and Declan, I might've been jealous.

Back in Rye, Annika zipped through the town, passing the turn-off to Zoë's place. Next, we passed the turn-off to mine. Then, the turn-off to school, and, to my relief, the turn-off to Jagger's.

"Where're we going?" I asked, no longer able to sit in suspense.

She smiled slyly. "I volunteer at the hospital."

I didn't like hospitals. I'd once waited in one for five hours, alone, after cabbing it to the emergency room when I'd cut myself with a knife. Especially now, I didn't want to think about lying to cover for my mother's absence, or the throbbing pain as I'd waited to get stitches, or being nauseated by the scent of my own blood. I especially didn't want to think about how she'd groused all the way back to our shitty apartment about how the hospital had called her anyway and said they wouldn't release me until a parent picked me up.

"You get to bring people to your volunteer gig?" I asked Annika. "That sounds...untraditional."

"Oh, today's not *my* day..."

Clearly amused by keeping me in suspense, Annika's lips twitched as she pulled into the hospital lot.

"I thought we'd drop in on a colleague. Tuesdays and Thursdays are Jagger."

Tuesdays and Thursdays. Volunteering at the hospital. Jagger's elusive disappearances were explained. Still...

"Jagger's a candy striper?" I almost shouted.

He'd made me insecure over being an afterschool volunteer? Annika looked like she was trying not to laugh.

"While I might pay to see him in a pink and white outfit, hospitals stopped having candy stripers, like, twenty years ago."

I wasn't laughing—I was still too busy being peeved. Her smile faded.

"Seriously, Roxy. You need to see what he does here."

I lagged behind Annika as we approached the entrance, wringing my hands all the while.

"I don't know if I can see him yet, Annika. What am I going to say?"

"Lucky bitch that you are, you won't have to say anything."

I followed her down a long hallway, up a staircase and down

a hall. When she punched a security code into a keypad next to a serious-looking door, I looked around to figure out where we were.

"N-I-C-U?" I said aloud. I had no idea what that meant.

"NICU." She sounded out the acronym as if it were a single word. "Neonatal Intensive Care Unit. It's where the babies who are too sick to go home stay to get better."

She walked through the door.

"Jagger should be just through here."

The idea of seeing him—if even from afar—terrified me. It didn't help my nerves that I still couldn't fathom what it was she wanted me to see. But his profile was unmistakable from the instant I caught site of him through the window. The mere sight of him clenched my heart. He stood with his back to me as his body rocked slowly, his tall figure a stark contrast to the collection of enclosed little beds that looked more like futuristic pods. He turned his body slowly, his lips moving as if he were talking, and it was then that I saw the bundle in his arms.

Holy fuck. My boyfriend is holding a baby.

I gulped as I looked over at Annika. "Please tell me that's not his."

She rolled her eyes. "He's a *cuddler*, Roxy. So am I. Remember? We're volunteers. Babies need human contact in order to develop properly."

But Jagger was magnetic, and before Annika even finished her sentence my gaze pulled back to him. Even the wrecked version of Jagger was beautiful. Despite dark circles under his eyes and anguish written on his face, his gaze upon the infant was loving. When Jagger reached out the back of a finger to tenderly rub the infant's cheek, the corners of my mouth trembled.

"Jagger...cuddles babies?"

I bit my lip to keep from sobbing, but I knew it would be of no use.

"Every Tuesday and Thursday. And he loves these kids, Roxy. The one he's with today—Nick—is going home on Friday. Jag's gotten really attached to him. But that's what we're here for, to get them nice and strong. Strong enough so they can go home."

Annika's voice caught at the last part, and it all snapped into focus. Why she would volunteer her time working with babies. Why Jagger would. My heart either broke a little or opened then, I didn't quite know which.

"Annika?" I asked cautiously. Her eyes were shining. "What happened to your baby?"

It took her a long minute to answer.

"She was born on August 15 of last year. I gave her up for adoption. Declan was with me when they took her. She was the most beautiful little girl I've ever seen and I named her Daisy."

By then we were both crying and in an unprecedented move, I stepped closer and wrapped my arms around her waist. She wrapped back and it felt strangely comfortable.

Thirty minutes later, I was at home, shut back in my room. But I still couldn't face the music until I braved the final frontier. *Instagram.*

I knew he'd tried to get through to me there. I had so much to tell him, but I still didn't know what I would say. My heart raced as I logged on for the first time since I'd turned off alerts four days before. A single look at my start page had me completely overwhelmed. Thirty-two private messages, all of them from him. Most of them seemed to be lyrics from songs. We had to talk. I knew we had to, but there were so many letters, and messages, and play lists and being kidnapped by Zoë, then Annika...it was all a bit too much. Some part of me screamed that we had to go back—to start again and do things right—to do more than apologize to one-another and pick up where we left off. Something about this mess made me want to unravel every wrong.

It has to be this way.

Through my tears, I clicked to compose a new message and typed his name into the recipient bar. Now it was my turn to send him the lyrics to a song.

> *I hope you know, I hope you know*
> *That this has nothing to do with you.*
> *It's personal. Myself and I,*
> *we got some straightening out to do...*
> -Fergie
> *I know we need to talk, but right now there are too*
> *many words. I'm sorry I can't handle it all*
> *right now. Soon, I promise.*

After hitting send, there was only one more thing to do, and I cried impossibly harder when I navigated to my friend list, scrolled to his name, and hit "remove".

TWENTY-SEVEN

CREEP

I wish I was special.
You're so very special.
But I'm a creep.
I'm a weirdo.
What the hell am I doing here?
I don't belong here.
-Radiohead, *Creep*

JAGGER

Nick stared up at me in wide-eyed wonder, his eyes registering a bit of alarm. In recent days, their hue had melted from deep blue-green to clear coffee brown. He'd mostly slept through my visits in earlier weeks, just after he'd been born. These past two weeks, he'd been more alert each time I came around.

Today, he was as awake as I'd ever seen him, and was giving me the infant version of a look I was sure I deserved. It said *"Dude. What the hell happened to you?"* So I told him. I told him everything that had happened since Thursday—he knew the whole backstory because I'd talked about Roxy before. By the time I waxed reminiscent about the day Roxy and I had stood on the seaside bluffs, I was certain Nick and I both looked ready to cry.

"She made herself so vulnerable that day. She laid it all on the line. She showed me why she was so insecure. And what did I do? I started kissing her to change the subject. That was the same day she asked me why I friended her. Why couldn't I have just been honest?"

Unsurprisingly, a six-week-old had no advice, but it was a good sign that he'd made an effort to stay awake. The kid could barely keep his eyes open any time I talked, so by the fact that he was still listening, I knew he cared. At some point, something made me look up and look through the window behind me. It was hard with the shaded glass. Apart from the vague outlines of the nurses at their station, I doubted there was anyone there.

At home later, another weird feeling came over me as I pulled up Instagram. Weirdness escalated to sheer terror the second I saw a message from her. For four days I'd waited for anything, but something wasn't right. Her name was right there, but there was only a blank picture next to where it said "Roxy Vega".

What the hell?

I clicked on her name, but it didn't take me to her profile. For some reason, it wouldn't link. I could only see the message. I read It once. Twice. The third time it finally clicked.

I tried to reason with myself, to allow myself to trust the words she'd written. *"I know we need to talk"* seemed promising. So did *"soon"*. But I noticed where she'd left off. And I didn't like the lyrics—not at all.

––––––––

I COULDN'T SLEEP, couldn't bear the idea that Roxy was making decisions, couldn't stand the notion that so much remained unsaid. Too few of the words I'd written to her these past few days had been mine. They kept me awake—the words that hadn't been said, the words I'd saved for the reckoning I'd hoped would come. But I was losing hope. Because tomorrow would make five days and teenage years were like dog years, so not talking to someone for five days felt like not talking to them for a month.

The longer I lay in bed, the more the words bubbled forth. And then I was sitting upright and a minute after that, I was at my desk. And half an hour later, I was scribbling a note to my parents and getting ready to walk into the garage. Five minutes after that, I was speeding down deserted roads in the middle of the night with the letter I'd just written on the passenger seat of my dad's car.

My Dearest Roxy,

I know I'm overstepping my bounds by writing this letter. In case this ends badly, there are things I need you to know. I know this may cost me whatever small chance I may still have with you, the only thing I'm sure of is that you deserve the truth. So here it is: my story. I guess you'll tell me how it ends...

Once upon a time, there was a lonely little boy who found he didn't like being around people. They looked at him strangely— with pity or envy or infatuation or some other unwelcome emotion in their eyes. He liked his parents (though for a time they didn't seem to like him), but he never had many friends. He didn't even have neighbors, given the sheer isolation of his big house in the woods.

As the boy grew, he found something to replace the loneliness that seemed like it had been with him forever—he found it could be conquered with music. When he played piano or listened to his parents' old records, he felt better. Not because the music took away his loneliness, but because it understood.

The boy grew. And his friend, Music, became the most impor-

tant one in his life. He eventually made friends, but never strayed from the only one that owned his heart. Something else happened as the boy grew older: it became more difficult for him to hide. Eyes turned in his direction were filled with pity, envy, and infatuation and he found he needed a new way to fight them off.

So he surrendered. He showed them everything they wanted to see, told them everything they expected. It was easier than showing them who he really was. Besides, Music was his, and he wanted it to himself.

Then she came.

He wished desperately to know her but had no idea how to reach out. So he admired her from afar. His friends knew how he felt about her (it was obvious to them) and one of them forced his hand. And the boy found that, with the opportunity to know her dangling before him, he no longer had the strength to stay away. So he did get to know her, and she was like him in ten different ways and better than him in twenty more. When he was with her, everything in the whole world felt right. She even made Music sound better.

The boy was so busy falling in love with the girl that he forgot an important thing: building his walls for so long to keep people away had made him forget how to let them in. And, even with this girl, for whom he'd laid bare the dearest pieces of his soul, there were many other pieces he'd forgotten how not to hide.

And, so he left those walls intact, hiding away once again, desperate not to overwhelm her with his secrets. But now that he saw what his walls might cost him, he clawed furiously to tear down the stones.

I miss you, Roxy. Please come back to me. I swear, I'm trying.

Jagger

My hands had shaken as I'd sealed the letter and written the words on the envelope meant for Roxy. They shook because I meant them. I had to stop hounding her if what she really wanted was to move on.

To Roxy

(The last letter I will write you, I promise.

If you ever felt anything for me, please read.)

I stepped out of my car and walked carefully to the door, not wanting to wake Mr. Vega. The man had knives and I was prowling around in the middle of the night.

My hand still shook as I lifted the heavy brass cover of the mail slot. Blood thrummed loudly in my ears as I kissed the envelope and slipped it through. My heart broke at the thought that this might be the last time I ever stood on Roxy's porch. Looking up at her darkened window, I silently prayed.

TWENTY-EIGHT

SOMETHING'S ALWAYS WRONG

Another game of putting things aside
As if we'll come back to them sometime
A brace of hope. A pride of innocence.
And you would say something has gone wrong.
-Toad the Wet Sprocket, *Something's Always*
Wrong

ROXY

Come on, Vega, I chided myself as I tapped my pen nervously against the kitchen table. Crunch berries had turned the milk in my barely-touched bowl of Cap'n Crunch a pale ballet slipper pink. It was time now—way, way past time—to face the music with Jagger. ButI had no plan and I could barely think. Writing a list seemed like as good an idea as any. With Jagger suspended, I could work on it all day and in class.

I'm sorry.

It was a necessary start. And I *was* sorry—for the hypocrisy, the overreaction, the silent treatment, and for walking away. He'd deserved punishment and maybe even a little humiliation, but he'd not deserved five days of this.

You still have a lot of explaining to do.

I couldn't gloss over this part. His "secrets" still needed to be discussed. I just wasn't sure how and when to bring them up. Especially given number three, the hardest one to say, the one I didn't want to think about at all:

I have a lot of explaining to do, too. Like, a lot.

...so much that I didn't know where to start. Part of me wanted to let it all ride, to let both of our shit unfold over time. But that approach might complicate number four:

I know it's only been two weeks and we're all kinds of fucked up, but I desperately want you back.

Based on his letters, getting back together was exactly what Jagger wanted. Would he still want it if he knew the truth? Because I was fairly certain he'd placed the Roxy he wanted on a pedestal, while the real Roxy was rooted to earth.

The phone rang—I ignored it—I was too deep in thought, and I knew that my dad would pick up. Half a minute later he stomped into the kitchen, looking annoyed as he handed me the phone.

"It's your mom."

I was already shaking my head by the time I mouthed a "no", but he gave me a look that threatened what would happen if I didn't take it. She, too, had been calling through the weekend but I'd added her to the list of people who I was ignoring. She didn't even wait for me to speak before she started talking at me.

"Rox-xy!" she whined in an adolescent voice. "Baby, where have you been? I've been trying to get a hold of you."

I groaned internally, not in the mood for this after the kind of week I'd had. My mother was the last person I wanted to speak to.

"You could've just called Dad if you were worried whether I was alright."

I didn't hide the irritation in my voice.

"Of course *you* were alright," she nearly huffed, with an emphasis on "you". "If you weren't, Lucas would've called."

I rolled my eyes, intent on hustling her off of the phone.

"Well, listen. It's been real and all, but I need to get to school. I've already missed two days so I don't want to be late."

I knew if she wasn't calling to make sure I was okay, she was having some kind of crisis. I also knew she wouldn't ask what had happened to me that had kept me out of school for two days.

"Something terrible has happened!" she exclaimed tearfully before her voice lowered. "I broke off my engagement with Adam."

I closed my eyes and took a steadying breath, anticipating the melodramatic display that was sure to come. She'd flipped her shit over lesser breakups, but this wasn't just some guy she'd been dating awhile—this was a publicly-announced engagement. Inasmuch as it had been her meal ticket to the rich and famous buffet, I was 99% sure it hadn't been she who broke it off.

Once upon a time, I would have simply remained silent, would have let her verbal diarrhea run its course. I would have offered her words of comfort and commiserated with her every self-deception, her every piece of flawed logic that rendered what had happened not-her-fault. I would have glossed over the commonalities among her relationship failures, agreeing that, indeed, she deserved better, knowing all along that she would repeat the same kind of behavior—again.

So what are you gonna do, Roxy? Take a stand for once? Or, let her make you pick up the pieces?

"I'm sorry to hear that, Mom. You seemed happy while it lasted."

Ignoring my brush-off completely, she commenced the verbal

diarrhea anyway.

"Yeah, well Adam's a lying sack of shit, just like all the others," she said, her voice now cold. "From here on out, Roxy, I am *finished* with men."

I am finished with men.

How many times had she said the same words? I'd once held out hope she'd make them true. If I was honest, my mother "finishing" with men had been my greatest wish when I was young. If she did that, I'd thought, she would finally choose me. But, fuck it —times had changed. In the eight months since moving to the town that I'd thought would bore me to tears, I'd bonded with my dad, made my first best friend, and fallen in love with a boy. My whole life in Rye had been a much-needed dose of normal, and I wasn't going back to crazy town with her.

"...but now that I'm back in L.A., we're gonna put things back the way they belong. Remember that street we could never—"

She prattled on, but I tuned out for an enraged minute.

What the fuck does she mean, "we"?

"I talked to the school, and they'll take you back any time. And guess what? I'm giving you my Accord so you'll have something to drive. I have a little money saved from what I made on tour—not as much as I'm entitled to, of course—but at least Adam's influence was good for *something*. Did you know..."

I seethed with anger. It was all too much. By the time she finished her absurd fairy tale, I had fallen deadly silent.

"Roxy?" she asked after a moment. "Baby, are you still there?"

When I spoke, it took effort not to scream. My teeth were clenched, my voice was a low growl, and the fist not holding the phone was clenched at my side.

"I'm not coming back."

"What?" The sincerity of her surprise incensed me. After eight months, it still did not occur to my facile mother that I was better off without her.

"I said..." My voice rose to dangerous levels. "Even if I hated Rye as much as you did, I would sooner run away than come back to L.A. to live with you!"

By then, I'd pushed back from the kitchen table and my voice had echoed loudly.

"Why are you being like this?" she sniffled, immediately the victim. "I called to tell you that I want you to come home."

I didn't care.that I was on my feet yelling at my phone that sat, face-up on the kitchen table, or that my father had just barreled back in.

"I *am* home, Mom! And if you knew anything you'd know I have everything I need right here. I have friends my own age, and my boyfriend is not a lying sack of shit. Sure he's got flaws, but he's an amazing person and I might lose him because of you!"

By the time my dad ripped the phone from my hand and took it off of speaker, angry tears raced down my face. Tucking me under a protective arm, he took over with my mother.

"I would send her to Judy before I'd let her go back to L.A., but in case you missed it, she likes it here. This conversation is over, Star. If you're stupid enough to sue for custody, I won't hesitate to provide the court with evidence of a few things I'm sure they would be eager to know. And I know you know exactly what I'm talking about."

I was too busy soaking my tears on his shirt to strain my ears and catch the other half of the conversation.

"Well, it was a mistake for me to let her go, too," my dad continued a few seconds later. "But, I got my shit together before it was too late for me to be her dad. If you want a relationship with her, I'd advise you to do the same."

Once again, I didn't hear her retort, though it sounded indignant from what little I could hear of her tone. But my dad gave as good as he got.

"You have no more control over whether or who she leaves

behind than anyone had over you. Don't forget—she's almost eighteen."

He clicked the phone off and set it—more like threw it—back on the table and collected me into his arms. We each caught our breath for a long minute until I sniffled a bit and pulled back.

"Aunt Judy?" I swiped at my eyes as I asked.

He gave me a mischievous smile at the mention of his ultra-conservative sister.

"You know how she feels about Judy."

Kissing the top of my head, he took a step back and gave me a serious look.

"You are the best thing in my life, kid and I would never take back having you. But I'm sorry I gave you Star."

I sniffled involuntarily and squeezed my eyes shut.

"What if I turn out like her?" I whisper-sobbed.

His hand squeezed my shoulder, which he shook firmly but gently.

"Roxx, the only thing you inherited from Star was her beauty."

I opened my eyes and new tears spilled forth. This time he wiped them away.

"I'd like to say you got all your great qualities from me. But the truth is you've always been your own person."

He wiped another tear, and I nodded weakly, half-knowing that it was true.

"I don't know what to do, Dad...to fix things with Jagger. I told him to stay away until I made a move, except now I have no clue how to make things right."

"He'd take anything, Roxx—you have to see that. And he didn't stay away."

Reaching into his back pocket, he pulled out an envelope written upon with Jagger's unmistakable script.

"He dropped it off in the middle of the night."

I raised my eyebrow in question, but my dad just shrugged.

"I was up."

I ripped it open as delicately as my thinning sanity could handle, reading it slowly, at the beginning from fear, but soon to caress and savor his unbelievable words. By the end, my eyes were blurry with tears, but I got the most important parts. His letter made me feel like the luckiest, most cherished, most unoriginal person on earth. I looked up, in earnest, for help.

"He writes me love letters, Dad. And sleeps on our porch. Did you know he knows how to write songs? I want to apologize, but I can't think of anything that isn't completely lame." I wiped at my eyes again, still looking up at my father. "What's the most romantic thing you've ever done, Dad?"

"Uh-uh, kid. Don't take lessons from me." He smiled wryly. "Nothing I did ever worked."

"Please," I begged. "I'm desperate. I've never been in love. I need all the help I can get."

My dad's eyes widened, and I realized I'd used the "L"-word. It sounded perfect rolling off of my tongue.

"The best advice Pop-Pop ever gave me was to forget about chocolates and roses. It has to be personal. You win a woman over by doing things that matter to *her*."

I thought about stolen iPods and Foo Fighter tickets and love song lyrics written on guitar-monogrammed paper. I remembered Skittles and Coke and toasted bagels with cream cheese and coffee with too much cream and sugar. I thought of passing notes in Civics and trading texts during class and writing innuendo-filled messages on Instagram. I thought of love letters and flowers picked straight from his mother's garden. That was where I had to start: with thinking of something that would feel sweet to jagger, just like every romantic gesture Jagger had ever done had been just for me.

TWENTY-NINE

TOTAL ECLIPSE OF THE HEART

And I need you now tonight.
And I need you more than ever.
And if you only hold me tight,
we'll be holding on forever.
And we'll only be making it right,
'cause we'll never be wrong together.
-Bonnie Tyler - *Total Eclipse of the Heart*

ELSIE MONROE

"JACK."

My eyes shifted from the sitting room entryway to my husband's reading chair. At the moment, he was doing just that, his nose in the afternoon paper. Either he hadn't heard me or he was pretending not to; the newspaper made it hard to know which. Slow, sad notes from Jagger's piano in the parlour below may have drowned out my voice.

"Jack." I hissed louder, leaning around the mica lamp and over the table that separated our chairs.

He looked up this time, bending the corner of his paper low enough for him to see my face. He looked sexy like that, brow furrowed in concentration as his reading glasses sat on his nose. Pushing that thought aside, I shifted my eyes back to the piano room and motioned toward it with my head.

Jagger, I mouthed, looking pointedly at my husband. *Listen to what he's playing.*

Jack pulled his glasses off and folded up his paper. I watched recognition cross his face as he identified the song: *Wild Horses* by The Rolling Stones.

"Do something," I said out loud this time.

He looked at me sadly and spoke with compassion. "This is what seventeen-year-old boys do, my love. They suffer from broken hearts."

But I shook my head. "I've been watching him all week. He's getting worse. I found him face-up on his bed this morning listening to *Ain't No Sunshine When She's Gone* on a loop. It's time to intervene."

He patted my hand in a gesture I was sure he meant to be soothing.

"Coddling him is only easier on *us*, love. He needs to learn to make it on his own."

Then my stubborn husband went back to reading his paper. I sat back in my chair in a huff, still worried about my son, wanting more to throw my book at Jack than to read it. I knew he was doing what he thought was right, but Jagger's vibe felt wrong. Heartbreak was part of growing up, but the music shouldn't hurt like this.

At some point, he transitioned into *Nothing Compares 2 U.*

Oh, God—it's getting worse.

My lips worried at my fingernails as Jagger's emotion poured painfully through his song. When it came to an end, I willed him to pull himself up off of his bench, to take a step towards whatever came next. But after a long pause, new notes rang out definitively. My determination to engage my husband multiplied when I recognized the song.

"Damnit, Jack, *listen!*" I whisper-shouted.

This time he folded his paper and threw me the same sympathetic-but-complacent look. I rolled my eyes and pointed exasperatedly at my ear. His face clouded over the moment he figured out the song.

"Is that *Total Eclipse of the Heart?*"

I nodded sadly, sure that his comprehension finally mirrored my own.

"Jesus Christ." He looked toward the door that led down to the parlor.

I saw in his eyes the moment he decided to take action.

"To the office, dear. It's time for an intervention!"

I rolled my eyes, but stood up.

No shit, Sherlock.

———

JAGGER

Bouncing in time with the music and working my fingers furiously over the plastic buttons, my video game guitar took the brunt of my aggression as I sang at the top of my lungs.

"And it feels, and it feeell-lls like, heaven's so far away! And it feels, and it feeell-lls like, world is so cold, now that you've gone away! Gone away...gone away. Yeah. Yeah—"

"—Son—"

"—Yeah. Yeah. Yeah. Oooo-ooooh! Oooo—"

"—Son!"

Whipping around in utter surprise, I saw that I hadn't heard wrong. My parents rarely came into my room without my knowledge but indeed I was not alone. My dad stood by my bed, remote control in hand, turning the music down.

Oh. I guess it was pretty loud.

After fiddling with the buttons 'til he gave up and turned the whole thing off, he strode back a step to wrap his arm around my mother.

"Sweetheart, we came to talk to you about Roxy," she began. "You seem to be taking it hard."

I'd seen in their eyes that this moment was coming. They were a united front.

"We love you, son. And we'd like to help you get her back. We'd like to offer our resources."

I plodded over to my bed and flopped down on my back 'til I was looking up at the ceiling. I'd been doing that a lot.

"Your *resources*?"

They were talking about money, but I couldn't see how that would help me win Roxy back. If anything, something too showy might hurt my case.

"You've been at home sulking for the greater part of two days," my Dad said a bit sternly. "It's time to get back on the horse. You're not the first man to be in the doghouse, son—now it's time to get her back."

I groaned. Because *I'd tried!* I wanted to shout it even more loudly than I'd been singing. Couldn't they see I'd tried?

"You need a grand gesture, dear. Grander than the others. We'll pay for you to move the piano."

I sat up then and looked between them like they were crazy.

"Move the piano *where*?"

"Under Roxy's bedroom window, of course," My Dad chimed in. "You'll write a song for her, then play it beneath her window. Play it 'til she comes out."

When I looked at my mother, she was smiling conspiratorially.

"Go all Lloyd Dobbler on her ass."

My parents looked so determined, so well-intentioned and driven to help, that I smiled a sad little smile. They sat on my bed, one on each side of me, cinching their arms around my back.

"I don't know," I mused. It did sound kind of perfect, but was it all a bit too 1989?

"She asked for space," I said miserably, trying not to cry. "Last night, she asked me to leave her alone. And I get it—I mean, I *have* kind of been stalking her, so..."

My Mom pulled my head onto her shoulder, and we sat in silence for awhile. I felt so much less bereft in the protective fold of my parents' arms. I was exhausted all of a sudden and I hoped that maybe tonight I wouldn't have any trouble falling asleep. When my Dad started telling me a story, it reminded me of when I was very little, and I let myself get lost.

"Did I ever tell you that before I met Mom, Nana wanted me to marry someone else? Her name was Lily—she was my best friend of fifteen years. We grew up together, and our families were friends. To Nana—and everyone else, for that matter—it was a given that we would end up together."

"When I met Mom at UCLA, I never told her about Lily. At the time, I told myself all kinds of lies as to why. Lily was beautiful, and we were close, and we shared private jokes, but things between us weren't romantic. The truth was, I didn't think Mom would understand."

"When I brought your mom home for spring break, it was a total disaster. Lily was supposed to be in Italy with friends but she cancelled at the last minute. Of course, she walks right into my parents' kitchen, confident and unannounced, and jumps on me to give me what I'm sure looked like an intimate hug. What happened next was like something out of a movie. Lily turned around to your mom and said "Finally, we meet! I've heard so many wonderful things about you."

My mother interrupted the story then. "And I said 'Really? Because I don't have the faintest clue who you are.'"

I winced, stealing a glance at my father and noticed his eyes fixed on my mother. I don't think I was imagining that, after twenty years, he still looked a tad sheepish.

"Mom caught the first flight back to San Francisco. I followed her, of course, but she wouldn't speak to me for a week."

I took a deep, shaky breath and sighed onto my mother's shoulder. It felt good, the way she was stroking my hair.

"I sent her flowers, made her mix tapes, made a little album of pictures from when we first started dating. But she didn't give me the time of day until I did something huge."

The sound of my parents chuckling was drowned out by a sudden blare of sound. We all started.

"What was that?" I whispered.

My heart beat wildly. Living in the middle of the woods made for a strict playlist of nature noises. This was not a nature noise.

"It's coming from underneath your window."

My mother sounded hopeful. I looked at my father, whose lips were curling up in a smile.

"Well, what are you waiting for? For God's sake, son—go see what it is!"

They both nudged me forward, and, on shaking legs, I approached the tall French doors that opened to the outside. The sound got stronger and a glow of yellowish light could already be seen beaming from the ground below. My face flushed hot and my heart drummed like a snare as my eyes adjusted to the dark.

"Roxy," I sobbed in relief and surprise as my eyes fell upon her form.

For, standing atop of the hood of her dad's truck, flushed and beautiful as ever was my one and only love. And, God bless her, the boom box she held over her head was half as big as she was.

THIRTY
I WANT TO KNOW WHAT LOVE IS

In my life there's been heartache and pain.
I don't know if I can face it again.
Can't stop now. I've traveled so far
to change this lonely life.
-Foreigner, *I Want to Know What Love Is*

ROXY

I sat at the end of the Monroe's long drive waiting for the rain to abate. A clumsy girl climbing onto the hood of a truck in a rainstorm balancing fifteen pounds of primitive electronics in tiny hands did not seem wise. With my luck, the unwieldy boom box would slip and fall on my head, effectively knocking me out. And I couldn't let Jagger try to rescue me again—this time it was up to me.

Peering down at the yellow legal pad with its purple ballpoint pen writing, I stared at a half a day's work. It had taken a come to Jesus with my mother, a heart to heart with my father, and hours of thinking to figure out what to say. I'd used half the notebook pages writing and editing, wordsmithing and crossing out. The page I stared at now was the final transcription. Yet, after so many drafts, I knew it all by heart.

Once upon a time, there was a scared little girl who wanted only to feel safe and loved...

Never had I dreamed that the stupidest lover's spat in the world would force me to take such a hard look in the mirror. I was nervous, of course, to share what I'd learned with Jagger when what I'd only just learned about myself felt fresh and new. But now was the time; Jagger deserved the truth; and, for him, I'd put it all on the line.

Speaking of putting things on the line...

I glanced in wonder at the boom box by my side. It had taken only an hour to find it in my dad's garage but a full four to track down the tape. I'd had the whole ride to Littleton to sort through my mental music files and pick out the perfect song. Once I had, I'd known I'd have to find some way to get it on audio cassette. I went to two vintage stores that I knew sold tapes, but found nothing that remotely fit. Half an hour at an internet café with no hits on stores selling cassettes and I was stuck with the tape that remained in the bay of my dad's box. Before resigning myself to the prospect of having to use something from the *Freedom Rock* album, I tried Freecycle and eBay Local as a last-ditch attempt, seeing if any random neighbor might have what I wanted. I nearly fainted when I saw where the tape was on auction for a modest starting price of $2.75.

Holy shit. It's at Plastic Fantastic.

I raced there as fast as my dad's truck would take me. Wet, frantic and no-doubt looking just a little scary, I made a beeline for the register and saw the face of the familiar clerk.

"Hey, you're Jag's girl!"

"Thank God you remember me," I breathed, practically collapsing in relief on the glass display case counter. "Listen, I screwed up with Jagger. I need to get him back, and I think you have something that could help."

I elaborated, telling him about the boom box and my crisis of lack of tape.

"Righteous plan, babe! Very *Say Anything*—good choice, going with the '8os. But are you sure you got the right song? What about *Hard to Say I'm Sorry* or *Can't Fight This Feeling?*" He waggled his eyes conspiratorially. "A little REO Speedwagon never hurt."

"I don't know..." I hedged.

"Ooh! I got it!" he exclaimed triumphantly, snapping a soulful finger and breaking into song. "I wanna take a little time...a little time to think things over...I better read between the lines...in case I need it when I'm older..."

Grabbing an unseen guitar from behind the counter and switching into the right key, he wailed into the chorus to "I Wanna Know What Love Is". Ready to burst into tears from the kind of day I was having, I stood there and let him finish the song. When he broke out of his reverie, he refocused on me. My face must've given it away.

"No?" he asked, wincing.

I just shook my head. He disappeared for a moment and returned with the tape.

"Then this is on me, babe. Not that you need it. Jag's totally in love."

I broke out of the memory when I noticed the sound of tiny pelts on the truck had gone silent, a sign that the rain had stopped. Looking back at my paper, then at my stereo, I started the engine on my truck. My heart rate doubled when I approached the house and saw his car parked outside of the garage. By the time I parked under the balcony off of his lit-up bedroom window, I was panting like an overweight dog.

It was no small feat for me to climb on my fender to scale the high-up hood of my dad's truck. Setting the boom box down and following it up until I, too, stood on the surface, I pressed the heavy play button and hefted the beast of a boom box over my head.

Here goes nothing.

The volume knob was cranked to the highest setting, and once the music started, the stereo shook with sound. But, I could barely hear the lyrics I'd so painstakingly chosen. I was too busy looking for Jagger.

A tall shadow beyond the curtains of the French doors barely preceded the doors flying open. Light from the room illuminated a wide-eyed, crazy-haired, slack-jawed, beautiful Jagger. I held my breath for seconds waiting, waiting, then strangled out a sob when I saw his lips mouth my name. Our eyes locked and I was lost. But I was lightheaded and it was dusk and I didn't trust that what I wanted to see was there.

And just like that, he turned on his heel and slammed the French doors shut behind him. Except my song hadn't finished and nothing that would have sparked hope had lit his eyes. My arms fell slowly from above my head, sinking down like me, until we were a pitiful pile of destruction knelt upon the hood.

I'm too late.

I didn't realize I'd spoken it aloud until his velvet voice spoke the sweetest answer.

"No, love—you're right on time."

THIRTY-ONE
OH SHERRIE

Oh Sherrie, our love
Holds on, holds on
Oh Sherrie, our love
Holds on, holds on
-Steve Perry, *Oh Sherrie*

JAGGER

My hands gripped the waist-high glass balcony wall as I peered down in relief at my girl. *This song,* I marveled. *She picked the perfect song.*

> *You should've been gone,*
> *knowing how I made you feel.*
> *And I should've been gone,*
> *after all your words of steel*
> *Oh I must've been a dreamer,*
> *and I must've been someone else,*
> *and we should've been over.*

Once my conscious mind caught up to my body, I was jumping down the stairs two-at-a-time and racing out the front door. I assured my love that she was not too late and collected her in my arms. I may have relished the scent of her hair and the weight of her body for minutes before I saw that she was wet, and probably cold.

"Please," I begged, looking down into gorgeous coffee eyes. "Come inside. Let me get you warm."

She shook her head stubbornly. It was hard to know whether the moisture on her face were stray raindrops or tears.

"It's my turn to talk."

However much I wanted Roxy to get inside before she caught hypothermia, now didn't seem like the time to insist.

"But I need you to just listen."

"I'll do anything you want," I breathed.

Nodding, she stepped back an inch or six, her hands holding fast to mine. The shaky breath she took before starting made me a nervous about what her story would hold. She read from a crumpled paper with purple writing.

"Once upon a time, there was a scared little girl who wanted only to feel safe and loved. Unlike luckier little girls, who had a mother and father to take care of them, this girl was mostly looked after by strangers. When she was very young, and she cried or had a bad dream, any of a long series of babysitters might be there to hear. Sometimes they comforted her, but they were no replacement for her mother."

She looked up briefly, gauging my reaction. I nodded for her to go on.

"But the girl's mother wasn't really like a mother at all, and she made it so that the girls' father couldn't be a father. Her life became about proving to everyone what she could be and never looking back. The truth was, the mother deeply resented the daughter for getting in the way of what she thought she should be. There were times the mother could barely look at her daughter for as much as she blamed the daughter for robbing her youth, and because none of it had been the girl's fault, it hurt."

She took another a shaky breath, keeping her eyes averted in something that looked like shame. My own stomach twisted with anger, but I put it aside.

"But the daughter survived," she continued eventually, a trace of strength reinforcing her voice. "Learned how to soothe herself. Learned how to make it through day by day. Learned important things her mother never taught her when she spent summers with her father. The mother moved them around a lot when she was young, so it was hard to keep friends. Left at home alone for hours on end, the small girl discovered music. It became her teacher, her friend, her shoulder to cry on, but most of all, her escape. No matter what apartment, or room she was confined to, she could always put on a CD."

"When the girl got older, the mother really disappeared. She said she needed to find the girl a father. But the girl already had a father, even though he lived miles away—what the mother really wanted was a husband. The men she brought home were sleazy enough to promise things they never planned to give, and the mother was stupid enough to believe them."

Finally, she met my eyes and I noticed her hands had started shaking. For a moment, I feared one of her mother's men had hurt her and, God help me, the very thought made me homicidal.

"And, so the girl learned to see the world: men could not be trusted and she would never be stupid like her mother. People who were supposed to care for her would abandon her, and she could only rely on herself."

"Oh, baby..." I breathed sadly, allowing my thumb to stroke her cheek. Bringing her hand up to meet mine, something bright lit behind her eyes.

"Then she met *him*. The boy who made her dare to wish

everything life had taught her could be different. He was beautiful and extraordinary and brilliant and more magical than anything she had ever seen. But she was invisible to him. He sat next to her in class every day, consuming her senses as he sat impassively for months and months, and paid her no mind."

I knew I deserved it, but *ouch.*

"Until one day, he did. And his attention gave her the most sublime feeling, but terribly bittersweet. Because everything she knew about men and boys and this boy told her it was too good to be true. So, when *that night* happened (the one that proved her theories), she'd been waiting for it all along. She knew a boy as magical as him couldn't possibly want her and that it had only been a matter of time."

I started to protest, but she took her finger to seal my eager lips. Shaking her head, she chided me gently. "My story."

So I let her continue. When she was finished, I'd say plenty.

"So she ran. Buried her head in the sand. Thought until her brain hurt. She had never seen until then how much a part of her this cynicism was, or understood that she was so jaded. When she came up for air, an amazing thing happened—the boy actually wanted her back. She'd figured out by then that she could trust him with her heart, and wanted to go running into his arms.

"But she didn't at first, because she was afraid he only wanted the girl he thought she was. She wondered, if he knew she was this messed up, would he possibly want her now? So she tried to let him go a second time, but found she couldn't stay away. Because in that short two weeks she'd known him she'd fallen hopelessly in love."

And just like that, my words from a moment before disappeared, and there was only one thing I needed to know.

"Tell me how the story ends," I choked.

"She devised an elaborate plan to tell him the truth and hope to win him back. Except she needs his help."

"Anything," I breathed.

"Be friends with her."

My face fell.

"*First.* Be friends with her first. Don't take her back until you're sure she's really what you want."

Oh, love, how could you think anything you tell me could make me change my mind?

"What's the second thing?"

"When she tries to make it all up to you, have pity and play along."

Before I could respond, she smiled sadly, planting a chaste kiss on my lips before taking the stereo and getting in her car. I touched my lips wistfully as her truck disappeared down my drive. In a daze, I ambled at a snail's pace toward the front door and collapsed on my own porch step. Beyond my own relief, I was heartbroken by her story, full of questions and speechless with lingering surprise.

She said she's in love with me.

My girl loves me.

She said she wants me back.

But, for now, we have to be friends.

She thinks I'll change my mind now that I know the truth.

Her story explained a lot—everything, really. It strengthened my resolve, making me determined to show her how different things could be.

Play along, she'd said. Except I'd wanted to act. I'd wanted to take off her beanie and run my fingers through her dampened hair, to tilt her chin up and kiss her deeply. I'd wanted to tell her I loved her and that we'd figure it out and to murmur my own regrets into her ear. I considered all of this as I stared out at the rain.

When the phone in my pocket buzzed, I pulled out the device. I'd kept it on loud mode since Saturday. The futuristic-

sounding echo that I'd custom-programmed on the phone indi-
cated a waiting message on Instagram.

*@Roxxy_roxxy_roxx wants to follow you. We need to confirm
that you know Roxy in order for you to be friends.*

I grinned like a lottery-winner. Without a moment to waste, I
hit "confirm".

THIRTY-TWO

I STILL BELIEVE

If there's one spark of hope
left in my grasp,
I'll hold it with both hands.
It's worth the risk of burning,
to have a second chance.
-Brenda K. Starr, *I Still Believe*

ROXY

Peering through the window of Zoë's car, I craned my neck to scan the Trinity High student lot, finding relief only once I was certain that Jagger had not arrived. Pointing to the corner section by the steps, I nearly waved my arms in impatience as I instructed Zoë to park her car as close to the spot where I would wait for him as possible. Zoë was having too much fun watching me get nervous about what I had planned.

Her car had barely come to a halt before I hopped out and grabbed the breakfast I'd brought for Jagger. He loved Golden Grahams even more than I loved Cap'n Crunch. Leaning against the back of Zoë's SUV, I balanced his breakfast on the flat part of the bumper in the back. Resuming the lip-biting that had gone on pretty much all morning, I scanned the road tirelessly for Jagger's car. So focused was I on scanning, I hadn't noticed Annika had arrived.

"Is Roxy channeling Gunther?"

Zoë giggled at Annika's remark. I ripped my eyes away from the road long enough to shoot her a look.

"You were the one who told me to go get my man."

Zoë clapped her hands excitedly. "Tell Annika about last night!"

I shrugged a little. "I played him an apology song on an old boom box. It was a little 1989, but I don't know...it was inspiring."

Annika studied my face in that calculating way before the corner of her mouth crooked upward in an approving smile. "Perfect."

Zoë looked impressed by the high praise from Annika. Before I could dwell on this, I sensed Jagger's presence, and found that his car was coming up the drive. I tried not to stare as he parked in a nearby spot, but by the time he got out and walked my way, I was ogling him—hard.

"Morning, Jag," I said, suddenly shy.

"Morning, beautiful girl," he murmured, stepping in close. "Are hugs of greeting permitted between friends?"

No.

"Yes," I whispered, breathless.

He bent to wrap his arms around me, lifting me up against his chest, holding me in a long embrace while my feet dangled six inches off the ground. His nose buried in my hair, his almost inaudible sighs of contentment, and the way every inch of his body pressed against mine were delicious reminders that we were so much more.

"I brought you breakfast," I said, as he set me down, and turned toward Zoë's back bumper.

I watched for his reaction. He smiled crookedly the second his eyes fell on the box.

"Golden Grahams?" He raised an eyebrow, but looked impressed. "Organic milk?"

I shrugged at the same time I produced my dad's plastic camping bowl and spoon from behind my back. "You're fancy like that."

He smiled softly. "This is incredibly sweet."

I shrugged again and he picked up the cereal as well as the quart of milk. Walking both of us to his car, he sat on his hood and I helped him help himself.

"Want a bite?"

"Oh, no." I shook my head.

He threw me a heart-stopping smile.

"Humor me, friend. You know how I love to feed you."

But Jagger and I could never be just that to one another. Maybe we never had been. Taking things slowly with Jagger would be harder than I thought.

————

JAGGER

It took a great deal of discipline not to use my tongue to clean the errant smudge of cereal-sweetened milk that had settled on the corner of Roxy's mouth. But I would play along.

As if Roxy could ever be anything less than my love, I thought, relishing her exquisite blush as I used my finger instead. From the slight slackening of her jaw as she watched me lick the dab of milk from my fingertip, I hoped she felt the same.

"Can I carry your books to homeroom?"

If you had told me three weeks ago I'd be letting a girl carry my books, I'd have driven myself to the hospital for a head check. But this was Roxy and her tiny apologies were endearing. I handed her my dark-green messenger bag and watched in amusement as she shouldered hers and mine. After she let me hold the doors open for her, I stuffed my hands in the pocket of my jeans.

"Did you sleep well last night?"

Our classmates studied us unabashedly as we made our way into the schoolhouse and down the hall. Small talk was a far cry from the flirting we would normally be doing.

"Like a baby. How could you tell?"

She smiled when she answered.

"You look a lot better than you did last night."

When we stopped in front of my homeroom, I couldn't stop the much-more-than-friendly words from flowing.

"Last night I got back something I lost."

She swallowed thickly, but didn't break our gaze. "I didn't mean to scare you. And you never really lost me."

"Good," I said gruffly, my throat constricting at the thought. "I hope I never do."

"Have a good day, Jag," she whispered, but didn't move. I was dying to kiss her lips.

"You, too Roxy." I recovered my bag, and smiled as convincingly as I could before entering the room.

Thirty-five minutes later, first period was dragging when my phone vibrated in my pocket. Being especially discreet as I checked for a message, I muted my grin when I saw the text was from her.

Roxy: 18-36-2

I had no idea what it meant.

Jagger: -20?

...to which she shot back:

Roxy: Not arithmetic. My locker combination.

I smiled, and quickly texted back.

Jagger: Danger is your middle name, Vega. Do you know what

I could do with information like this? (Hint: raid your secret Skittles supply at will)

My subdued laugh earned me a glare from the teacher. I wiped the smile off my face. It was only my second day back since the end of my suspension and I was in enough trouble as it was.

When the bell rang, I took my time gathering my stuff and slinging my bag over my shoulder. There was no reason for me to hurry since my next class was right next door.

"You told me the Skittles were a lucky guess..."

My head shot up at the sound of her voice. Her first and second period classes were in a different building. She looked slightly winded, as if she had rushed to reach me so soon, which, of course, made perfect sense.

"I pretended not to know you loved Skittles so you wouldn't think I was a stalkerish freak. But, Roxy, I won't lie to you anymore."

Then she surprised the hell out of me.

"I know you won't. I gave you the combination to my locker because I trust you."

And suddenly it clicked.

"If it's any consolation," she continued, walking towards me and the middle of the room, "some of my own actions might have been considered to be slightly stalkerish as well."

"Is that so?" I raised a hopeful eyebrow, walking towards her myself until we were separated by only a desk.

"Only if looking at all the photos you're tagged in on Instagram, like, a thousand times, qualifies as stalkerish."

"Oh, Miss Vega, it most certainly does. But it's nothing compared to how obsessively I checked to see whether you had updated your status."

We stood there for a minute, kind of smiling at each other, until she closed the distance between us by walking around the desk. Instinctively, my head dipped, my face gravitating towards hers, though I managed to refrain from acting on my almost-constant need to taste her lips.

"Isn't it nice?" She held me prisoner with gorgeous, imploring eyes.

"Isn't what nice?" My voice was suddenly gritty.

She reached out her little hands to slide my messenger bag off of my shoulder.

Smiling sadly, she said, "The truth."

THIRTY-THREE
ALL OF ME

What's going on in that beautiful mind?
I'm on your magical mystery ride.
And I'm so dizzy, don't know
what hit me, but I'll be alright.
-John Legend, *All of Me*

ROXY

Unsurprisingly, the entire student body quieted down the second Jagger and I strode, together, into the cafeteria. Between our conspicuous absences and the Dan Wesley incident, our relationship remained under a microscope. We'd gotten stares all morning and folks were no doubt dying to know what was going on. And our current arrangement was bound to cause even more confusion.

Though Jagger had technically respected my "friends for now" request from the night before, it was clear that maintaining this boundary was difficult. He couldn't keep his eyes off of me, his hug that morning had not been innocent, he'd come *this close* to kissing me twice, and it wasn't even noon. It gave me sick satisfaction that he was having so much trouble, but the truth was, so was I.

Which is why you have to follow your plan of letting the whole truth come out. He has to be as rational as possible when he decides.

"So we were thinkin' about heading up to Littleton after school since the posse's back together," Gunther started once Jagger and I arrived at the table. Deck, Annika, and Zoë were already there. "See a movie, maybe grab some dinner?"

"Actually...." Jagger cleared his throat, looking nervously at me "Thursday is my volunteer day at the hospital. I go there to cuddle babies."

Three jaws dropped.

"You told me he was an orderly!" Declan exclaimed, glaring a little at Annika, who just rolled her eyes.

"Dude, babies?" asked Gunther.

Meanwhile, Zoë clapped her hands together and exclaimed "You cuddle babies? Jagger, that is just too sweet!"

Heedless of the other reactions, Jagger looked at me as if to say "See? I can be an honest guy." A smile bloomed on my face and then one took to his and I was soon sure we sported matching goofy grins.

"It's almost as sweet as the work Gunther does at the hound puppy rescue!" Zoë gushed, linking her little body under Gunther's arm and snuggling in close to her man.

Gunther looked both sheepish and mildly defensive as he shrugged. "Those little guys need good homes."

Not wanting to embarrass Gunther, I ate a tater tot to hide my smile. It really was extremely cute.

"Dude, puppies?" Jagger mocked good-naturedly, play-punching Gunther in the arm.

Not wanting to be left out of all the adoration being heaped on his friends, Declan finally chimed in "I slip the dirty old geezers porn when I volunteer at the old folks home!"

Even Annika cracked up at that.

————

JAGGER

Seeing as how I'd missed so much school, I should've been paying attention. Yet I found that all I could focus on was the heat of Roxy's body next to mine. It was a wonder I knew anything at all about civics for the way she had always broken my concentration.

...like she's doing right now

Though we sat side by side, I missed playing with her, missed our banter of exchanged texts and passed notes. But I gave her her space. After all, it wasn't as if she were ignoring me. Each time I was tempted to flirt, I reminded myself the difference between winning the battle and winning the war.

While scribing a particularly incoherent notation from Mr. McAbee's droning narrative, I caught a moving scrap of notebook paper out of the corner of my eye.

I have a confession to make.

When I glanced at her curiously, she looked sheepish. Pulling the paper back to her side, she scribbled another note and slid it over.

I knew about the cuddling. Annika told me, and I kind of watched you in action on Tuesday.

She bit her lip in nervous anticipation of my reaction. I wrote back quickly.

I thought that was you.

Her jaw slackened slightly at her surprise at my answer. Now it was my turn to pull the paper back to my side and scribble another note.

Roxy, when you're near me...I can feel you. On Tuesday I got the feeling I get when you're around. I thought it was just wishful thinking, but...

Her expression changed and I worried that I'd done it again. While she sat, unmoving, for a long moment, I berated myself for still being fail on the difference between welcome honesty and creepy TMI. I might not have breathed as I tried to sneak glances as she penned her response.

I know what I said last night, but...we really need to talk.

My heartbeat quickened at her note, and at the look on her face. "We really need to talk" did not sound good. For the first time since she'd shown up beneath my window, I was scared. Paranoid, perhaps, but I didn't trust my hands not to write a desperate plea for our talk not to be "the breakup talk" so instead I simply nodded. But, we didn't break eye contact. Indeed, our look was the most intense one we'd ever shared. It melted from unreadable to vulnerable to Roxy's special brand of determination.

"Mr. Monroe, Ms. Vega, under normal circumstances I'd have you consult your lab partner to catch up on the material you missed. But, since you've both been absent for the greater part of the week, I strongly advise you to *pay attention.*"

I slid my gaze away from hers, even though not being able to read her was like cutting off my blood supply. If not for Mr. McAbee's reprimand, we might have gazed at each other like that for the rest of class.

———

ROXY

Ten minutes after the end of Civics, I had traversed the quad and was slipping into the woods. Jagger's abilities had proven themselves again and he had dazzled the powers that be. That we would only miss his study hall and my gym made me slightly less guilty about practically demanding that we talk.

I wasn't immediately sure what had happened back there, only that his comment had set something off. By measure of truth-telling, the friendship plan was progressing as it should. It was only the sub-plan—the one that dictated that I not fall in love with him any harder in the process—that was blowing up in my face. Some part of me really did want both of us to start telling the truth. Yet, whereas my truth would probably drive him away, his truth was making me fall harder.

If he leaves me, I won't survive.

Not wanting to be seen disappearing into seclusion together, we were staggering our retreat. I walked back pretty far, past where the stoners went to get high, past the large boulder everyone called "makeout rock". I didn't worry about getting lost, or about Jagger knowing where I was, for I could hear his soft footfalls closing in behind me. I stopped in a clearing of fallen trees, waiting until he was so close I could feel his breath.

"I can't do this anymore," I whispered. "I thought we could be friends, but, I—I want to be more, but I can't 'til you know the truth."

Wringing my hands, I gathered the courage to turn around and face him. His sage-colored eyes were a storm of pain, hope and fear. His hands were stuffed in his pockets and his demeanor reminded me of a person who was bound.

"You still want to be more than friends?" he asked uncertainly, his voice mirroring the emotion in his eyes. "I'm trying so hard to be honest with you, Roxy, but sometimes I'm afraid the truth of how I feel is exactly what's scaring you away."

I took a terrified breath and prepared to hit Jagger with the ultimate act of honesty: cutting all the other bullshit and telling him what I was really afraid of.

"It does scare me," I whispered. It was all my weak voice

would allow. "Only because I'm afraid it's the things I let you believe—the things that aren't true—that make you like me so much. And I think if you knew all of me, you may not like me at all."

He stepped an inch closer, his eyes softening a bit, though he had not let down his guard.

"So tell me, Roxy. Tell me all the things you think will drive me away. But I already know the outcome. Nothing will change the fact that I have fallen completely in love with you."

It hurt me to hear him say the words, injured me to think he might rescind them once he knew the score. But there was no turning back, so I surrendered to what I had come there to explain.

"I'm damaged goods." My voice still failed to manage anything above a whisper. "The story I told you last night only scratched the surface. Being with you—even seeing your parents together—showed me that everything I think about relationships is backwards. I tried to be a good girlfriend, but I didn't even last a week without totally freaking out. And I'll probably screw up again, too."

He was standing so close, peering down at me with intoxicating intensity.

"I'll forgive you," he said with frightening conviction.

My voice chose that moment to re-emerge, shaking peculiarly in protest as it rang.

"This is serious, Jagger. It's worse than you think. You know the whole thing that started our fight? I gave you hell because Declan friended me, but the truth was, it wasn't even me who accepted the request—it was Zoë."

He didn't even flinch.

"If you could, would you undo what Declan and Zoë did?"

I shook my head.

"Then I don't care."

I scoffed in disbelief.

"Would you care that I judged you for being a manwhore, when I'm far from innocent myself? People here assume I'm a prude, but I fooled around with boys in L.A. Like, a lot."

But the expression on his face didn't change.

"What do you want me to say, Roxy? That this makes me think less of you? I always knew you had secrets. Don't you get that I love you because we're the same?"

I couldn't breathe.

"The depth of your eyes, the sadness in your smile..." He whispered the next part. "...your music...before I met you, I didn't know there was anyone else like me."

He was even closer now, his body ghosting against mine, his fingers gently stroking my jaw.

"Before you, I couldn't remember the last time I really laughed. Or wrote a song, or hoped that my life could be like this."

His eyes had softened to something so heartbreakingly vulnerable that I let my own fall shut. And just when I thought I would implode from not being able to contain my emotion, he wrapped his arms around me before I tore myself apart.

"I don't care how many skeletons you have in your closet," he choked out in my ear. "I see your beautiful heart and I just want you to love me back."

I let out a breathless sob as I hugged him in return. The wetness on my temple wasn't rain. I whispered, just loud enough for him to hear,

"Don't you get how much I do?"

EPILOGUE: THINKING OUT LOUD

People fall in love in mysterious ways.
Maybe just the touch of a hand.
Me I fall in love with you every single day.
And I just wanna tell you I am.
-Ed Sheeran, *Thinking Out Loud*

TWO MONTHS LATER

THE FORECAST WAS for an unprecedented seventy-two degrees, a veritable heat wave for May in Rye. On any other warm Saturday we would have already been somewhere worshipping the returned sun, but today was the one day this spring that Trinity High would become a test center for the SATs. That's how me and every other junior bent on getting the hell out of this town found ourselves spaced strategically far apart among the long library tables. We filled in tiny ovals with #2 pencils when not staring longingly outside.

If the graph of the function f is a line with slope 2, which of the following could be the equation of f?

I remembered the $y = mx + b$ rule and looked for the right answer.

y = 4x - 2

y = 2x + 4

y = -2x -2

y = .5x +2

y = -.5x + .5

I filled in the oval corresponding with the second answer. Looked like all those hours that Roxy and I had spent studying in my room had paid off after all.

Roxy. My eyes shifted toward where she was sitting, near the front corner of the room. That I was flying through the test gave me time to study the line of her profile. For a long moment, I took slow survey of her concentrated brow, the way her mouth played at the end of her pencil when she wasn't writing an answer, and that damn beanie she would probably still wear even if she had on a bathing suit and it was July.

"Eyes forward, Mr. Monroe," scolded Mr. Taylor, the proctor of the test and the only teacher at Trinity High impervious to my charm. Roxy glanced back at me briefly, upon hearing my name, which, of course, made me smile. I winked flirtatiously. She blushed, and I could see the subtle upturn of her lips. I smiled more widely before we both went back to our tests. Mr. Taylor rolled his eyes. I didn't care what he thought of us, or teenage love, or making goo-goo eyes at one another during a serious test. I didn't care what anyone thought, because I knew. I knew Roxy was the best thing that had ever happened to me and that moving here was the best thing that ever happened to her. I knew this summer would be epic. I knew college was a long way away. And I knew that, one day, I would marry that girl.

———

AUTHOR'S NOTE: THE MUSIC

Thank you for reading! This story has a very long history that I talk about in detail on my blog. I love nostalgic music, and I love awkward teenage love. Growing up, I was kind of like Jagger and Roxy: heavily influenced by the music my parents listened to and most likely to hang out with other kids who respected the old jams. The year I graduated from college, I turned down a more sensible job to work in the music industry. Spending my early twenties getting paid to interview bands I had idolized and be backstage at shows was pretty awesome.

I've lost count of how many songs are mentioned in this book, but I did create a playlist. If you want to listen to the songs on this book, find me on Spotify by searching for Kilby Blades.

Also, if you like my writing, please consider joining my mailing list—it's the only way to read extended previews of my upcoming titles, to get freebies and outtakes of my stuff, and to win giveaways of other books I love. If you just want to hear me overshare about my crazy life, follow me on Instagram. Most importantly, follow me on Amazon so you'll always know about new releases, and while you're doing that, why not leave a review so that other readers know what to expect?

And speaking of knowing what to expect from my other books, I'm known for what critics and bloggers have called "feminist romance". My books feature empowered heroines and multi-dimensional heroes who are staunch advocates for their women, stepping back from their own spotlights in order to let their women shine. In my angstier books, my characters are dry-witted, but my lighter ones serve up a ton of humor. All of this in the midst of delicious dilemmas and never-before-seen plots. I write across audiences as well, from Young Adult, to New Adult to Contemporary to Steamy Romance.

HERE'S WHERE I THANK PEOPLE

I would be remiss if I didn't take a moment to thank all of the people who helped this book come together. Sarah Latchaw was my original beta reader on this story. I was such an admirer of *her* book, *Hydraulic Level 5*, that I approached her out of the blue for help writing my very first novel-length story. Her generosity in giving me clear, tough-if-I-needed-it feedback on how to think about my characters and move my story forward set an invaluable standard in my life as an author.

Elizabeth Mackey of Elizabeth Mackey Graphics must also be thanked. This is the fourth amazing cover she's designed for me and I'm looking forward to more.

I'd also like to thank the huge crew of author-friends and fans who kept me sane as I slogged through many slow iterations of this story. This is the very first story I wrote but, as you may have noticed, I published it fourth. There are so many people who were along with me for this journey that it seems impossible to mention all by name. Please know that your support meant, and means, the world to me.

ABOUT KILBY BLADES

KILBY BLADES IS A FRESH NEW VOICE in smart contemporary romance. Critics laud her "feminist fiction", noting empowered heroines and multi-dimensional heroes. Her debut novel, "Snapdragon", was a ten-time finalist and a five-time winner for honors including the HOLT Medallion, the Publisher's Weekly Book-Life Prize, and the Foreword Indie Award. She has been nodded for a total of twenty honors for her complete library, including a win for Best Debut Author in the 2018 RSJ's Emma Awards.

When she's not writing, Kilby goes to movie matinees alone, where she eats Chocolate Pocky and buttered popcorn and usually smuggles in not-a-little-bit of red wine. She procrastinates from the difficult process of writing by oversharing on Facebook and giving away cool stuff to her newsletter subscribers. Kilby is a citizen, a social-justice fighter, and above all else, a glutton for a good story.

facebook.com/kilbybladesauthor

twitter.com/kilbyblades

instagram.com/kilbyblades

bookbub.com/authors/kilby-blades

goodreads.com/kilbyblades

ALSO BY KILBY BLADES

FICTION

Snapdragon

Chrysalis

The Art of Worship

Worst Holiday Ever: A Family Drama Romance Anthology

Worst Valentine's Day Ever: A Lonely Hearts Romance Anthology

–

NON-FICTON

Marketing Steamy Romance

The Book Marketing Audit (2019)

CPSIA information can be obtained
at www.ICGtesting.com
Printed in the USA
LVHW052318111219
640173LV00007B/1217/P